$\mathcal{V}$OICES OF THE $\mathcal{S}$OUTH

SLAMMER

ALSO BY BEN GREER

FICTION
Halloween
Time Loves a Hero
The Loss of Heaven

BIOGRAPHY
Presumed Guilty: The Tim Wilkes Story

SLAMMER

BEN GREER

LOUISIANA STATE UNIVERSITY PRESS
BATON ROUGE

Copyright © 1975 by Ben Greer
Originally published by Atheneum
LSU Press edition published 2002 by arrangement with the author
All rights reserved
Manufactured in the United States of America

11 10 09 08 07 06 05 04 03 02
5 4 3 2 1

Library of Congress Cataloging-in-Publication Data

Greer, Ben.
    Slammer / Ben Greer.
        p. cm. — (Voices of the South)
    ISBN 0-8071-2789-2 (alk. paper)
        1. Broad River Valley (N.C. and S.C.)—Fiction. 2. African American
prisoners—Fiction. 3. Prison riots—Fiction. 4. Prisons—Fiction. I. Title.
II. Series.

    PS3557.R399 S57 2002
    813'.54—dc21

                                                                        2001054905

The paper in this book meets the guidelines for permanence and durability
of the Committee on Production Guidelines for Book Longevity of the
Council on Library Resources. ♾

For my mother and father

. . . for in those days the Broad River separated two Indian nations, the Catawba and Cherokee, and was called by both Awahuppidai—the line between the waters.

ONE

I

H E left the lonely warmth of the car, pulling his hat tighter, and squeezed between the other cars, side by side and still warm, too, in the darkness. From the city a great train, one-eyed, roused and rumbled across frosted tracks, across the marshlands and mean tobacco farms and poor dirt of Carolina, grinding toward this place. Beyond the barbed wire he could see a few lights in the buildings. He walked toward them while the night, garnered by the unseen river, rolled out through the low country, deep into the woods of pine and oak, far and wide to the sea.

Barbed wire and lights and, between the lights and the wire, cats. Crossing in and out of shadows, their eyes catching and releasing the light. The main gate rose over him. The train wailed against the north wind and the river was filling fast with darkness.

The wind whistled around the tall guntower, which looked empty, but he knew it was not. A guard would be sitting there now, one who came in the dark and left in the dark. Men had been killed by shots fired from this high tower. The late September wind ripped around the great buildings' corners and grated against his clothes. Tomorrow he would wear two pairs of socks. Gathering his wallet and loose change into one hand, he went up the steps and pressed a small brass button. The door opened quietly and he walked into light, heat.

"Morning, Walsh."

He nodded, blinking.

"Getting kind of cold out there, ain't it? There's a touch of fall in the air. Look at your oaks. They'll call it first."

Aaron Walsh emptied his pockets onto a counter. Took off his hat and spread his legs for the search. He turned and held Officer Carl Brantham's eyes. Brantham's face immediately caved into a grin. Taking Walsh's hat, he rammed a finger around the inside of the brim.

The Gateroom was narrow, with a high ceiling and bright lights, and smelled of ink and peppermint. There were four steel doors. To Walsh's right squatted an ancient switchboard and before it a wooden counter holding pens and directories and a Mason jar of peppermints. The pine boards of the floor were a foot wide. The walls were clean plaster.

Brantham's hands were moving on him now, across the top of the shoulders, under the collar, down the sides from the armpits, gently at the crotch, and then

4

spinning down thighs and calves to wring free at the ankles.

"Clean," Brantham said. "Better get you a hot cup of oil, huh?"

Nodding, Walsh filled his pockets and straightened the wrinkles in his uniform. Brantham barked an order into a microphone and a steel door slid open. Walsh moved through and approached the first gate. He could see the officer in the control booth, his face asleep in his hands. But, hearing Walsh, he reacted, moved, and the heavy gate swung open.

Now three flights of stairs down. Smelling the morning prison—eggs and coffee and fatback cooking. And beneath this the odor of the dark buildings and the men still sleeping in them. At the second set of stairs stood another gate—Carter's gate. Named for a guard who had been stabbed to death there some years ago. Walsh stepped down the last flight before the Tunnel. He glanced at a large sign above him: "Prison Is a Highway Not a Dead End."

Muscles tightening, gut beginning to clot. Mouth of pennies, as eyes and heart and brain all marshal and sharpen. Now at six o'clock, here in the first and lowest depth, he was awake and alert. Two hundred yards left and right of him ranged the long gut of the prison —the Tunnel. Connecting all buildings. Directing every man to the cell blocks. The walls were green; the floor, black tile. Neon lights made quick, white, acute light. Walsh knew if something should happen, the Tunnel had only two exits: one to the Yard and the one he had just come down. He walked to a rugged iron door and shoved it open. Quickly, a few faces glanced up at him,

5

then the officers smiled, nodded. They sat packed about small tables—some still sleep-ridden; most holding their faces quietly above coffee mugs, stunned as they always had been and would be by this descent.

Walsh picked up a tray and looked closely for cockroaches and grease. "Two easy over, Tailpipe," he said to the man at the stove.

Tall, black, and agile, nine years ago the cook had raped a high-school girl and beaten her brains out with a tailpipe. He dashed eggs onto the griddle, where they were swallowed in grease and the dark residue of other fryings.

A small room cluttered with tables and chairs, most of them sway-backed, mended with long bolts and plasters of tape. Everything food-stained. Windows and silverware running with steam. This room's only color, the wall mural, was painted in blues and greens and yellows, finished a few years ago by a prisoner. Pouring stuffing and a fine spiraled smoke from its neck, a turkey sat surrounded by moats of creamed potatoes and gravy and green beans. All this on an enormous platter, amidst dunes of sand and palm trees, the sun and a turquoise sea. The officers avoided looking at the mural this early.

The cook dredged the eggs from the griddle and slapped them into a plate. "That do it, bossman?"

Walsh ladled up some grits and sat down at a table with two other men. They were talking. Mixed his eggs and grits and listened.

"Always happens this time of year, too. Just about time the cold starts cracking in the air. Trouble hauls itself in." Sergeant Joe Creekland speaking, short and

6

bald. Large brass keys hung about his belt and rattled when he spoke.

"It'd be easier in the summer, not having to stand out in the cold and all. Not having to deal with them with one hand in your coat," Langford Cays said. A handful of boxtops lay on his tray.

"My wife says she gets messages about them, chills. Says she can feel them packing together. Maybe she's right. It's only when they start gathering we got trouble. One or two we can handle. But let them get in a pack and all they do is think of how to get us."

Lieutenant James Rhiner sat down next to Walsh. He heaped a piece of bread with red jam. "How your feet this morning?"

"Blisters," Walsh said.

"You hold on here another couple weeks—they'll get use to it."

A challenge, Walsh thought. He would hold on alright. Longer than any of them could guess.

"Trains maybe," Cays continued. "A lot more this time of year. Maybe they sneak in at night on trains."

"Too many apples, dumb ass. Hell, those cars are up to the ceiling with winesaps. All that fruit just cooling on down to the coast."

"Well, they're coming in at night somehow," Cays said. A long, gangly man with a limp, turkey nose. "I never seen them on the road. *Gypsies*! I never seen them bringing that fair in. Something kind of funny about that. Kind of—scary."

"My wife, she hates all the trouble they haul in. Stealing, cheating. All the filth they leave behind. But she'll make me take her. Oh, hell yeah. First frost and

7

she starts looking forward to that damn gypsy fair."

Creekland turned in his chair, his keys rattling. " 'Course maybe our new warden don't want us to have our regular day off for the fair, huh, Walsh?"

"Wouldn't know," Walsh said.

"Wouldn't?"

"Naw," Walsh replied, making the word sound as country as he could.

"New warden, new man. Sounds like a nice, shiny team for poking around in things."

"Now how long's Warden Cates been here, Creek?" Rhiner interrupted quietly.

"Eight months longer than he should have been," Creekland snapped.

The other guards listened, watched.

"And how long you figure the Chief's been here?" Creekland said, mocking Rhiner's tone.

"Freeman's a good man. He's tough."

"Twenty-three goddamned years and *he* should have been made warden. Not Cates. Not that book-learned boy who starts messing around with things he shouldn't!"

"Talk to the governor," Rhiner said.

"You one of Cates's men now?"

Rhiner set his cup down easily and traded stares with Creekland.

A clatter and someone cried out. John Snipes's hand shot to his mouth. Blood. All turned. Snipes waved everyone away. With his right hand he pulled a tack out of his mouth and set it in a spoon for them to see. With a handkerchief he wiped his mouth clean. The men who had not finished breakfast pushed their plates away. Some even put their coffee down. Walsh recon-

8

sidered his eggs and grits. Decided not to eat here again. Wondered why he had begun eating here in the first place. To fit in, he knew. To let them grow used to him. Even drinking their debilitating coffee, instead of honey and tea. He was on the front lines here and doing alright.

"Must have worked loose from the sack," Snipes said.

Some of the guards looked for Tailpipe, but he was gone.

"Roll call in two minutes," sputtered the squawk box.

Guards rose to put on their hats, rattling change and checking their green uniform jackets for cigarettes.

"Powdered glass next time," someone said.

The Countroom—big and damp and filling with cigarette smoke. The guards forming into sloppy lines. Walsh nodded again to the men he knew, but did not speak. A man clapped him hard on the back.

"Little too much stump water last night, huh, boy?" Gus Williams, controller of gate six, and even this early his face shot red with whiskey. "Bet it was that damned Kentucky Rose, too. Rusty razor blades and shoat corn —you can't beat that mash." Williams laughed, hacked deep in his chest.

Walsh squared his hat. Williams and his friends did not drink on the job, but in the morning they had a shot or two just before they came in. It helped them. Some took pills through the long day, uppers and downers. If there was ever trouble . . . Walsh thought.

Chief Freeman was standing before them. Tall and broad, white-haired. He always appeared quickly, letting no eye catch him coming. He smoked a big twenty-five-cent cigar. Jesse Cates had been brought in and

9

made warden over Freeman, who had been second in command for a long time. Walsh felt the bad blood between them, felt a choosing of sides among the guards.

"Good morning, gentlemen," Freeman said.

The guards came to attention, tucking away conversations and bellies.

"Today's assignments are the same. You're at your regular posts. I'm a man short for the Count. Volunteers?"

No one moved.

"I'll pick someone out later. Anything to add, Mr. Rhiner?"

Rhiner shook his head.

"All right, gentlemen, let's take her down."

Smiling to himself. Such a typical expression—let's take her down. So indicative. But somehow he had to get close to Freeman. Close to real power here. The best way was to volunteer, but he had to be careful. Pragmatism and compromise. He remembered when he first applied for the job, only two weeks ago, how Warden Cates angled easily into the room—a hill boy with an M.A. in psychology who was short and red-haired and, so Walsh was told, always carried three guns on him outside the prison, including a .44-caliber derringer in his sock. Rhiner was asking him some questions when the Warden interrupted:

"Only one thing I'm concerned about, mister." He pointed out a window to the double fences running around the prison, the killing zone. "You're in a tower and you see somebody's butt crawling up one of those fences and you're holding a shotgun. Now what's your move?"

10

"Blow his ass off," Walsh said flatly. Knowing that he could not even point a gun toward another human being.

"That's my man," the Warden said. "That's my boy." Then he looked at Rhiner. "Now you're going, Jim. Those that pick good, get picked."

Walsh walked away from the others to stand by a wall. Already, he had developed what these men called "butt itch"—a fear, an awareness of his back to anyone. Relieved only by being in scratching distance of concrete.

The rest of the guards passed by. Walsh could still smell the whiskey. He moved toward Chief Freeman.

"Yard men don't usually count, Mr. Walsh."

"You said you were a man short."

Freeman glanced at his clipboard, then back at Walsh —tall and dark-haired, with quick green eyes, a white, sharp-boned face, and restless hands. "Very well. Buildings Two and One."

Walsh said yes sir, then followed the other Count men, who moved down the Tunnel in a loose knot. Some began taking off their jackets, loosening their ties. Not laughing or joking as the Count bells kept ringing. Walsh listened. They made no sound, moving. In a quiet current, they moved through the Tunnel, at the Tunnel shack took Count sheets from the third-shift guards, who always laughed and joked among themselves. Because they worked at night when everything was locked up. They always looked neat and carried shiny black lunch pails. Once, when they left games scattered around the shack and laughed loudly, Lieutenant Rhiner ordered Walsh to miscount. The third shift had to stay until the Count was right. On that morning they had stayed three extra hours and worked some for a change.

Today the third shift could not find the keys again, which happened once or twice a week with them. The first-shift guards cursed under their breaths and spread out from the Tunnel shack. Apart from one another, blew their noses or lit fresh cigarettes or hummed quietly to themselves and rattled their brown lunch bags.

Walsh looked out an open window to see the Yard, dark, very quiet, except for the wind which seemed to climb down from the towers. Prowling in the Yard like something more than darkness. A careful wind, not like the high, salt wind of Portland which had blown him a hard and clean Maine woman, with big hands and wide, strong thighs. Whom he left there . . . But that at least for now had passed.

The keys were found. The Count began. Walsh ducked into a steel door that led to Cell Block Two. Two men counted a building, one the upper floor and one the lower. Walsh took the upper. Another guard opened the ward door and locked it behind Walsh. The turnkey waited for trouble. Most of the prisoners were awake, studying Walsh, waiting for the order.

"Count time!" he yelled, feeling his heart pound. Trying to stare levelly across the sixty bunks of men. Slowly they rose and formed the line. Walsh tried to think of the system—how he hated the system that threw men into cells, made them go through all of this—but he couldn't. Again the prisoners started making the noise. A sound low in their throats while they hit him hard with their eyes—testing, probing.

"Count time!" he yelled louder. The noise ceased and

he counted down the line and back up. Seventy-eight. He wrote the total on his Count sheet. As he turned his back, some of the men began breaking the line before he had left the ward. He should have stopped them, but he didn't have the guts.

The guard tending the door let him out. "You shouldn't allow those men to break line," he said.

"Okay."

"You'll get a shiv one day letting them break line."

Walsh turned in his count. "I'm counting in Building One now," he said to the night lieutenant.

"Got a light?"

"No, sir."

"You'll need a light. They're all in cells there. Take this one. It's red. It's all I got." He threw Walsh the flashlight.

Walsh walked down the Tunnel toward the door that led to Cell Block One. Angry with himself for still being afraid here. Trembling. Wondering when he would toughen up. His father had worked such jobs without trembling. Had not been afraid to stand with blacks and migrant laborers and miners. Even sacrificing his law practice for a vision. A chemistry that aligned his soul entirely with the oppressed. Yes, it was soul. Then the strike at Peppertown, Tennessee, and a stray shot that hit him and somehow drained his fine strength. And the years swung in fast, did not allow him second wind. Now he only drank and wrote angry letters to the *Daily Star* about the rights of workers.

But something of his old man bundled through Walsh now. More than blood and will. Something more. Begun in Maine. With his friends who had just jumped into the

13

car one night and driven north. Sick of college and high on sunshine. Ending up in Portland where they rented one of the big hill houses. Papaya juice and peanut butter by the wood stove. Hard snows piling against the dark house. Steaming chowders and guitar blues.

In Portland that restlessness he felt in college grew into something. Rice and Lewis busted for stealing a jeep, winding up on Kittery Island. And when he saw that place, what stone and mortar did to men, he knew where his stand would be. And he knew, too, that only a few had the blood. Now returned, a beginning in this prison. Wondering when he would toughen up.

2

"BLESS me, Father, for I have sinned . . ."

He closed his breviary, quickly slipping the stole about his neck, offering up his own unworthiness to God. The red light should have flashed on when the penitent kneeled, but it had been taken out some years before. The hole was filled with a plaster flower because the priest before him had thought red signals were old-fashioned. *Probably some kind of forty-year-old flower child.*

Father Edward Breen gave his prayer of blessing. In the middle, his stomach rumbled and he thought quickly —*maybe one poached egg.*

"I have sinned by missing Mass a couple of times, and by cussing and drinking, which I knew was wrong. By gambling away most of the money my wife sent me, and generally by not behaving myself as I know I should.

And Father, for some reason lately I been worrying about dying a lot. Maybe we could talk about that. And for all the things I may have forgotten, I'm sorry, too."

. . . the point is to keep up your strength, so maybe a couple of eggs, fried potatoes . . .

Father Breen balanced his face upon three fingers and leaned into the window. "Not bad, buddy. Pretty good confession. At least you're thinking. That gambling, though—you got to cut that out. Your wife could use that money, I bet. Now, about this dying business. Worrying about that's a waste of time, see? So why are you doing that?"

"I don't know, Father."

"You don't know. All right, I'll tell you why. Because you're thinking about yourself too much, see—the big 'I.' So think about something else. Girls, baseball, your neighbor. Let me ask you something. How much did you eat for breakfast?"

"Huh?"

"For breakfast this morning. How much did you eat?"

"Oh . . . a little grits, coffee."

"That's all, huh?"

"A piece of toast maybe."

"It's all right, just wondered. Now, about dying—when do you think about this mostly?"

"Night, I guess."

"What do you do at night?"

"Read."

"Read what?"

"Mystery stories."

"That's kind of stupid. You going to daily Mass?"

"No, Father."

16

"Okay. Start going to daily Mass and cut out the cops and robbers before bed. Got it?"

"Yes, Father."

"Ten Our Fathers and Hail Marys for the poor souls in purgatory, a couple for you and a couple for me." Breen bowed his head, passing a strong hand over the window. He could not feel that strange light, fire that he had once felt and thrived on.

"Thanks, Father."

"Right." His stomach rumbled again. *Guess I should cut the crap. A couple slices of toast. A little tea is all.* He waited a few minutes, to be sure there was no one else, then unwrapped his stole, kissed the cross at the border, and hung it on the crucifix.

At the seminary, which seemed so distant, as if never really a part of him now, they had practiced confession once a week. He remembered, after each penitent, hanging the stole back on the bloody, dusty feet of Christ. His friends asked why he didn't leave it on. And he said that in real life the stole was like a magnet. It grew heavy with sin and it was better on the feet of Christ. Some laughed and others were angry. They said he was too dramatic and that it's only a piece of cloth, Ed, and you're just trying to be spectacular and that's no way to make bishop, Ed. *This new kid probably doesn't even believe in confession, much less wear a stole. Well, the hell with him.*

He looked at his watch—7:25. A couple minutes of confession left. Clicking on a small reading light, he tried to concentrate on his Greek Testament, then flipped the newspaper out from his habit. He had underlined: ". . . P. G. Carter, convicted of grand larceny, was

17

sentenced to two years at the State Correctional Institute." Two years, hell. Five at least he should get. And this kid really had the moves too. Good legs, quick hands. An all-state running back once. But only two lousy years. The prison team would just get used to him. The courts screwed up everything. He stuffed the paper back into his habit and picked up his Greek Testament.

"Damn participles," he muttered.

A cold blast of air whistled through the cement blocks. As usual, he had rolled down his long black socks and hoisted his habit. An old trick good Father Ephraim had taught him. "The confessional is always assaulted by two things—sinners and draft. It is good to embrace them both," he had said.

He pulled the habit to his ankles and decided that if he was going to cut it down to toast and tea, he might as well cut the whole damn breakfast out. He resumed skimming the Greek. What he should really have was something simple, but nourishing. Like—lentils. If anything, that was what he should have for breakfast. As a matter of fact, that's what he should eat three times a day. Why the hell not? It was done once by the Fathers of the Church. It could be done again. Lentils. He smiled to himself. He could empty those damn cabinets and give all that stuff to the prisoners or something. He could probably save a hundred a month, pay off the new tires, and even lose part of his belly. *Then lentils it will be, and maybe three or four extra laps around the track, too.* A man sworn to poverty should not have a gut!

The chapel bells were tolling seven thirty. He turned off the light, blessed himself with holy water. He put a square of cardboard back over the bowl to save a little

18

from evaporating. When he rolled up his socks, he noticed the hair on his legs was disappearing. Fifty years old already. *Saints preserve us! They never told me about the hair.* He said a short prayer before the tabernacle. The new wooden altar smugly stared back at him. *Looks like a saw horse. A plywood offense to God.* But the Council had decided that all must see what the priest was doing at all times. He knew that the people did not pay any more attention than before. Good Pope John—Lord keep him—had let something else into the Church besides a little fresh air. She had fewer and fewer converts every year. The confessionals were empty. Deleting Latin had weakened the bonds of the Church in this world of treachery. *Now without this loving brace, corruption begins to divide the Body of Christ and burrow into the Sacred Heart.*

This new young man—whoever he was—had better see that, too. But he was probably like all the other new men the seminaries were turning out. Half-assed philosophers. Full of milk and sugar, Sartre and Camus. *Holy Mother!*

Six feet four, two hundred fifty pounds, and Boston-Irish, Breen had come to the prison sick of parish bazaars and Sunday night bingo. He had wanted to return to the missions in Brazil, but the Provincial said younger men went first. So he waited and every year for the past four received the same letter: wait, be patient, give younger men their chance. The hell with that. And now they were sending him this . . . "assistant." He wondered.

Breen blessed himself at the chapel door, went out into the courtyard. He tightened the cincture about his

19

Franciscan habit and moved up the stairs into the rectory, which was directly connected to the prison as was the chapel.

High in the guntower above, a guard was oiling his sights, strolling out on the gunboards.

Just inside the door, Breen took a deep breath. The good smell of the rectory: hot coffee, books warming by the radiators; the most delicate smell of oils and chrism. If anything, there should be an odor of corruption, despair. For Chief Freeman had told him that fifty years ago this room had kept the child molesters. They had been separated from the other prisoners then, and lived out their sentences. When Breen thought of these men, which he tried not to do, it was with a great hopelessness, a dark sense of dread. Sometimes late at night, or in a fallen moment of quietness when the rectory settled and creaked, he could picture it as in a dream.

Gray and ravening, they lay in their cells, hearts wild as rats, dreaming of dark things. One dreaming of some child he has watched at the seesaw all the long, hot day. Waiting in the dark stand of pines, weak from hunger, listening to the school bells, marking the time, listening to the last farewells as the child walks slowly toward the silent pines in wrinkled pants and shirttails. By the barefoot creek he binds the small hands. By the running water he does his dreadful work. . . . And all the night long they run for trains, always pulling ahead in dark iron and sparks, while the dogs screech relentlessly behind. Many nights awaking here, believing the knife still in their hands; in darkness and from these very rooms, howling at the waning moon. . . .

At Mass he prayed for their suffering. At Mass he

remembered their souls. In a way, it was a miracle that, after a few coats of paint and a few years, there was nothing left here but a shudder. It was the way the Lord worked, Breen knew. Quietly, simply, with paint and time, this and all things were repaired and brought to good order, perhaps someday restored and renewed.

In the kitchen, he poured himself a glass of orange juice, looked at his itinerary sheet. A typical day: rounds through the hospital, piled up bookwork, bills to be paid, Mass to be said, a quick sweep through the shops and, in the evening, the chaplains' meeting. *When he comes we'll see what kind of mettle the seminaries are turning out.* Today, he had only one real appointment: James Moultrie was circled in red, "bad ass" scrawled beside the name. *Slugged a guard in the county jail, huh? Let him try it with me.* Breen was putting the pitcher of juice back in the refrigerator when he saw the eggs and bacon.

After the slab of bacon had finished browning, he emptied out some of the grease and dumped in the eggs. *The point is . . . to keep up your strength . . .*

3

DANIEL Childs still dreaming in Building One, until a red light breaks through the bars, fills his eyes, brings him to.

"Count time," the guard says.

Throwing back the covers. Darkness, receding dreams. Why the red light?

"Let's get it to the bars. Let me see two hands."

Cold stone, dirty, sticking his hands through the bars, trying to remember things.

The guard moved on. Childs stood waking, then turned on his light, squeezed into the small space between the sink and his bunk. He looked in the mirror and ran a finger across both sides of his face. Blue eyes, a strong chin. Built lean and broad. By the sink stood a bottle filled with a dark fluid. He poured some into his hand and rubbed it into his cheeks. Making a face because of the bad odor, he held his nose and breathed with his mouth, and his eyes ran. The dark fluid dried and he wiped it away. *Two weeks is not long.*

The mirror reflected his cell: a bunk fastened to the wall on one side and supported by two chains on the other—no springs, just peach crate board and a thin mattress; the stool by the barred window; the bare stone walls. Above the bunk were four holes as big as quarters. Childs glanced at them in the mirror. Here they were joked about as the beginnings of an intercom system for the cons, or for the lenses of cameras that would determine the number of their masturbations for the sociologists. The other men made jokes about these things, but Childs did not want any sociologists watching him doing anything.

He pulled his socks from the bars of the window. He had heard that the bars were filled with ball bearings and that they could not be sawed through. The older prisoners had told him these tales, and he believed them and promised never to try and cut through the bars. Most of the glass was missing from his window, so he had stuffed it with paper and one old sock. The sock had a big hole, so he did not feel bad about it. He would have used shirt cardboard, but it cost twenty-five cents. Already in these autumn days he could feel the cool draft pouring from the cracks. John Hawkins, his new friend, told him that in winter snow would blow in. He liked that idea. John Hawkins said it would fill up the stool. He did not believe that. But he liked the snow. The stool squatted closely and seriously into the corner.

Outside his cell, he could hear the bells ringing his

23

cell block to breakfast. But he was not hungry and decided to take his shower now. Showers were required three times a week. Two days before, he had taken one in the nighttime. He determined that he would never do that again, that it was very stupid. Walking through the dark, wrapped only in a towel, he had heard the whistles cut through the air like knives. At first he whistled too, but then he stopped. The first time, he had not known how to dress for showers. He wore all his clothes and the men laughed. The next time he wore only undershorts and they whispered and made sharp eyes at him. Now, he wrapped the towel about his waist and put on his shower shoes. He banged on the cell door, yelled: "Twenty-seven!" After a few minutes, the tier boy came to his cell.

"Shower."

"Speak up, man." He was black and wore sunglasses.

"I got to take a shower."

The tier boy opened the lock and slammed the door into the wall.

Childs knew he should be nice to tier boys because they controlled the cells in his building, like the ward keepers did in the newer buildings. A man was not supposed to be out of his cell unless he had a pass or was going to or from work or the showers. Though he had been here only a week, Childs knew that the tier boys would let you out if you gave them a present sometimes. But if you got caught at the entrance to a building or in a shakedown spot without a pass, it was bad for you.

"What's your name?"

"Childs."

"This your first shower?"

Childs hesitated, his face crumpling. "I—I guess."

24

"What you mean—you guess, man?"

"I took some before this."

"Any this week, man? Can't you understand English?"

"I took some last week. I haven't had one this week yet."

"That's all I wanted to know, brother."

The tier boy looked at him slant-eyed. Childs knew he was annoyed. He was sorry.

"Twenty minutes. I got it marked."

"Alright," Childs said. He made sure his cell door was locked.

He lived on the fifth tier and had learned how to keep his shower shoes quiet. Most of the men had gone to breakfast. A few watched him from their cells. Soon he had to paint his cell. They told him he could use any color, and he picked blue, and they said it would be fine.

On the first floor, he noticed the men did not go straight to their jobs as they had been doing. They were collecting in small groups, though they seemed to say nothing, only stood close to one another. Now and again a guard broke them up.

Today he knew there would be much garbage. He hoped the cooks didn't throw out any rotten fruit because of the bees. But he was glad to have his job because he knew many men didn't have one. He made sixty cents an hour.

The water in the showers was rarely shut off. The showers sounded like a tiny storm beating in the corner of the first floor. Childs hung up his towel, quickly approached one nozzle.

"That don't work," a voice said.

Childs could hear some men soaping and scrubbing.

25

Because of the steam he could not see them well. He moved to another place.

"That don't work either," the same voice said.

He tried the handle and it did not work. Their lathering stopped. He could hear only the running water. Felt shy and cold and didn't know what to do with his hands. The shadows were deeper at the far end of the shower and he moved toward them.

"I'm finished," a man said and passed toward the door.

Under the soft bell of water, Childs felt protected, grateful. He would have thanked the man, but he was already gone. The floor was cold. The water was warm, and he washed himself clean without soap. Soap cost twenty cents.

Most of the men finished before him. He came out and went to his towel. Two men that he could not see were speaking in big whispers in the shadows. Childs was afraid they talked about him. He dried off, cinched the towel around himself, and went up to his cell.

Putting on his clothes, he wondered where he could get the paint. Someone tapped on the bars. "Yeah?"

"You said you'd do some sewing. It's just a couple of buttons—cross-stitching."

Childs took the clothes. He smelled perfume. The white man who stood outside was tall and thin, with sharp eyes. His name was Montana Red, and Childs had not known him long. "There'll be a lot of trucks today. I don't know when I can finish them."

"Any time will do. No hurry."

Montana Red watched him silently. Childs looked at the clothes. They smelled sweet.

"Want some gum?" Montana asked.

"No." Childs looked up, his face wide, free.

"You take your shower this morning?"

"Yes."

"You can always tell. It's a good smell."

Breakfast bells ringing in the other buildings. Down below, this building filling with the voices of men coming from breakfast, going to work.

"Garbage has a bad smell. Sometimes it makes my head hurt real bad."

A rhinestone glittered in one earlobe of Montana Red. "I want you to know, Danny, any time you need help, you tell me. I can do things here. I want you to always remember that."

Childs smiled. His blond hair shone. "You come by in a couple of days. I'll have them ready."

"Okay. Thanks." Montana Red stared at him a moment and left.

Childs put the clothes on his bunk. He looked at the buttons. *It will be easy.* He took out his sewing kit and began the mending. He remembered his parents just after the trial. His old country lawyer had shaken his bald head and said that he was very sorry and that he never thought that it would end like this. His father came up then and said softly that he'd write and would make sure that the rods and reels stayed in good shape. He said that they had some real good stuff now to stop rust, and you just remember you're always my boy. He hugged him close, then pulled away. Even now Childs could smell the cloak of tobacco and homemade beer that was always about him.

He put in three good stitches. Now he saw his mother

27

sternly looking him in the eye and telling him to be a man and not to let her down, that he had obligations at home and to hurry and get through with all this business, and give me a kiss, and he did. As always, she kissed him hard and on the mouth. She had always believed in being hard with him (so that he would be tough, she said) even when he was very young. When the doctors said he would never be normal. Never see or talk because of something that went bad in him while he was in her belly. But they were wrong. And the first day he could remember seeing her, she stood in the back yard of the mill house wringing the heads off chickens. Her hands were streaming with blood and the blind bodies raced around and thumped into him while their heads blinked big, golden eyes in the sun and their black tongues curled in the dirt.

On the first floor, the whistle was blowing. *They are early today. Today there must be many big trucks.* He put away his sewing kit. He hoped there would be no fruit.

4

J A M E S Moultrie was sweating in the great kitchen between the boiling pots, stirring the bubbling tomatoes. Like all new prisoners, he had spent his first ten days in the Detention Block.

Then the walk down to his cell. The guard's fist jammed hard into his spine . . . smelling disinfectant and sickness and cigarette smoke, which veils the face of every light bulb, making the halls and cold cells seem dark, red . . . through the endless gates strapped in bars, worn bolts, here and there set ablaze with a new stainless steel lock . . . hearing the heavy door slam behind him—all the world. One blanket, no shoes or socks, timid heat that whines through the pipes late at night, driving wide-eyed rats from the walls; the hunger, the darkness, the silence that paces in the stone corners watching him, never releasing him, except for a squeaking hinge, or the high, thin screaming of the Gospels deep within some other darkness, or the scutter of his food tray beneath the iron door, or the night howls of the guard dogs set loose in the killing zone. But he had endured it all, even the prideful, insolent visit of the priest. He had endured it all.

A tall cook lumbered up to Moultrie, carefully sizing him up: big arms, thick shoulders and neck, hard hands and eyes. "Reckon you know what to do with them tomatoes by now?"

"I know." Moultrie moved back from the big pot. An elevated ramp rose above it and the other pots, which were scorched at the bottom, gas fires burning there. He opened two boxes of salt, one of pepper, and poured them in. The pepper stung his eyes. With a wooden oar he stirred.

"That ain't enough," the cook said. "We let these boys know they've had a meal." The cook tugged off his cigarette and dumped in another box of pepper. Flipped his cigarette butt in and stirred it down into the pot and laughed.

Moultrie said nothing.

"Your buddy's on sausage over there. When he gets finished, you two take the handtruck on down."

The cook swaggered away, like all big, fat white men. Cocking his head from side to side, his big belly strutting out in front of him, with one fat white hand holding the other on his useless flat butt. They made him sick. Moultrie stepped down a ladder and crossed into a smaller room. Four men standing around a long table, making sausages. One of them was Lyman Donaldson,

30

nicknamed "Spoons." He and Moultrie had gone to school together in Atlanta. They had read books and carefully watched the news. It began with a lunch counter sit-in. They saw the oppression in the streets and so had begun their protest. Things did not go well for them. The people would not respond. Then they met Dr. King and caught fire. Moultrie had even been to his house once. They ate supper together and Moultrie was there for over four hours. Later, he felt ashamed for that night, for he did not hear what Dr. King said, only watched his eyes and his hands and wished to reach out and touch him. King had liked him and taken him on some of the marches, and when they gunned down that good man, Moultrie went out on his own. He and Spoons teamed together. And Moultrie had learned something that King never knew. A little violence, sometimes, was good. It helped people see. But King could not have known that. He was too good. The world was not meant for such good men.

The whites had put him here because he tried to help his brothers. He had put them together to make them strong, to gather what they needed, and the whites called it armed robbery. But he had seen his people wasting in the streets, and so he moved, believing he had the power to save them. Here, too, he saw his brothers wasting. Here, too, a black man was the Judas goat. Feeling that he had been chosen to come here, he and Spoons had made their plans. Moultrie was not afraid.

The sausage was heaped in big bowls. The men shaped it into patties. These were fried on long trays and the men who tended the frying wore special glasses because the fat spat at them.

31

"You about finished?"

"Yeah," Spoons said. He made a few more patties and put them on the tray. He was small and had one bad leg that scraped across the floor in a metal brace. Five years ago a motorcycle crash had crushed the leg. Moultrie called him Spoons because the brace made such a racket.

"The man says we take the truck down," Moultrie said.

Spoons wiped his hands. In an outside hallway they picked up a handtruck, pushed it down the Tunnel past steel security doors spaced about thirty feet apart, each one leading to a particular building: cafeteria, library, infirmary and, farther down, the cell blocks.

Near the end of the Tunnel, Moultrie spotted an old guard slouching behind several columns of pipes, apparently half asleep.

"There's an old one," Moultrie said, gesturing toward the guard.

"Chief Freeman. Been here thirty years."

"Looks like he spent twenty-nine of them sleeping."

"You don't mess with him, Moultrie. He's a strange guy. They say years ago he used to be a hunter. Bears mostly, up in the mountains. Story is two guys murdered his son. Cut the kid's guts out and skinned him in the woods. When they got life, Freeman signed on here and for the next ten years watched them. Every move, man. Got to learn everything about them. Knew where they were every minute in the prison. Like he was tracking something down. But always letting them know he was watching, waiting. They say he had plenty of chances to grease them from the towers, but never did. One slit

32

his own throat. The other one went nuts. So the story goes. But he ain't sleeping, man. Ole Freeman knows more about this prison than all three shifts of screws."

Moultrie looked back toward the pipes, but Freeman had disappeared.

A guard let them into Building Two, where the infirm and old were housed.

Spoons pulled the truck to one side and began taking out plates and silverware. Moultrie glanced about the ward. Across the ceiling, formations of steam pipes drove into the walls, some of them leaking at the joints, mended with ragged socks and rubberbands. From these pipes hung sharp aggregations of coat hangers, wet clothes drying there. Dressers stood by hard metallic bunks. The dressers were cluttered with medicines, inhalers, ointments, and salves. Crutches and wheelchairs and bedpans lay beside the bunks. A weak sun loitered about the drafty windowpanes.

On dry feet the old men moved to the truck, feeling its warmth against the frost of their bones. They filled their plates and returned to their beds.

"Lucius Smith," Spoons said. "He's the only one."

"Let me do it," Moultrie said. He fixed a plate and went to Lucius Smith, who lay in his bed. Black and frail and sunken away.

"Well, morning here, old man. How about some of this chow?"

Lucius Smith did not answer, his eyes half closed, nesting in his face.

"Hey, come on now. Let's try just a little, huh?"

He did not move.

Moultrie set the plate down and pulled the covers to

33

Smith's waist. A bad odor. Smith's bedclothes were stained with food droppings and urine.

Moultrie turned to Spoons. "Who did this, man? Who's responsible?"

"Screws."

"Get me a pan. Get me some goddamned towels, hot water, and a pan!"

Moultrie sat down easily on the bed. Ran a hand gently through the old man's hair, across his face.

Spoons returned with towels and a bowl of hot water. Moultrie dipped a towel into the water, wrung it dry, shifted it from hand to hand, letting it cool. He slipped it across Smith's face. The old man's skin seemed to turn blacker with the water, smooth as river rock. Moultrie washed Smith's neck and chest and slowly the old man came awake, eyes opening.

"Morning, old man. Time for you to be up," Moultrie said.

"Boy, if you going to speak to me, talk so I can hear you!"

"Morning," Moultrie said toward his ear. "We got you some breakfast."

"They's always breakfast this time amorning, boy."

"I bet you put it away real good."

"You try to put me away and I'll cut your ass, mother!"

"No, no. I say—I bet you still eat a lot."

"Hell, no, I don't eat a lot. Don't you know nothing 'bout old folks? What's the matter with you, boy?" Lucius Smith looked at Spoons. "What the hell's the matter with him?"

Spoons shrugged.

34

"In the morning, I take my coffee. That's all I want in the morning. That's all this body needs," Smith said.

Moultrie staring straight into his smoky eyes. "Then why don't you get up and get it?"

"What?"

Moultrie set the plate on another bunk a few feet away. "Why don't you get up and get your plate?"

" 'Cause I need my crutches for one thing and can't see good for another and . . ."

Spoons touched Moultrie's shoulder. "Wait a minute, man. You can't make him get out of that bed. He—"

"Shut up," Moultrie said. He grabbed Smith by the hands.

"Here, boy, what the hell you doing? You better let this body alone!"

Moultrie's face became very strong. "You can walk."

The men in the ward turning to watch, Moultrie feeling them, knowing he has the power to do this, feeling it burn in his hands.

"Moultrie, you're crazy, man."

"You shut your mouth!"

Moultrie moved away again. "Walk to me, Lucius Smith. There's a cable from me to you."

He moved a little closer. "Walk to me, Lucius, you can do it. Come on."

"Hell," Smith said, folding his arms over his chest.

Moultrie went back to him. He held both of Smith's hands and squeezed. "You can get up, Lucius Smith!"

"Boy, you don't know what the hell you messing with. Let loose of this body fore it slaps shit out of you! I'm tired, boy. What you trying to do to me now? I'm tired," he said, suddenly very sad.

35

Moultrie whirled to Spoons. "Put your hands on his head. Just keep your mouth shut and put your hands with mine."

They wrapped his head in their hands. The men began to gather about them.

"Press hard. *Hard,* goddammit!" Moultrie put his face an inch away from Smith's.

"You're going to walk, Lucius Smith! In my hands there's something to make you walk and I'm *squeezing,* oh Lord, I'm *squeezing* it into your head. Oh Lucius! You going to walk like you never done before."

Slowly, like an old and contrary lock, the worn face began to open, change, the thin body moving to Moultrie's rhythm.

"Lucius, oh Lucius, you going to throw away the crutches! Oh, them crutches you going to cast away, and rise up, yes and oh, yes, let them bed covers fall away, and let that crippleness fall off your bones, yes! Oh, Lucius, yes, you got it now! You're free now! Come on up, Lucius! Rise up! Oh, Lucius, rise up!" Moultrie stepped away, gleaming sweat.

Lucius Smith's face becomes alive, independent of the body. Slowly, he comes up, his arms struggling against the bed, his face wild, his mouth slack and drooling. A hand goes out for the dresser. One for the bedstead. A flopping under the sheets. Then, suddenly, he falls like a stone, knocking over medicines and glasses of water, a black heap on the cold floor.

Moultrie was looking at his hands, wondering at their sudden coldness.

"I tried to tell you, Moultrie. He's paralyzed, man," Spoons said.

36

The men about them stared. Some laughed. Most did not. The men turned their backs to finish their breakfast.

"Well, let's get him up," Moultrie said quietly.

Smith was humming an old song, not noticing anything now. They put him back in bed and covered him up.

As Moultrie went back toward his cell, he knew he could have raised Smith if he just had concentrated more, willed more. He knew he could raise them all off this white earth and plant them in the heavens like stars if he wanted to. That he had the talent, power, and he needed only to drive, drive, drive!

"Spoons, can you get me the meeting?"

"You sure you want to go through with this?"

"I have to move first."

"It'll be hard. I'll try."

"How much real support does he have?"

"A lot of guys work for him, man. Dope, ass, liquor. The Muslim's got it all."

"But some of his boys want to split up, right?"

"That's what they say. He's ripping off too much," Spoons said.

"When the cut-off comes, the pushers will yell a lot. Maybe try to get rough."

"You move slow, Moultrie. You watch. This place ain't like the streets."

"Maybe. But I'm going to treat it like the streets. I'm going to cut out what's ruining my brothers."

Moultrie did not like Building One. Smelled too much of white men. He could see them about him as he and Spoons went up through the cell block. He hated the way they talked. Hated the way the words slid out of their

37

long, skinny necks. His father had talked to him about digging up bodies for transportation across the state line. Once or twice, the coffins had broken open and the bodies fell out—all soap. The ground had made them into soap. His father said that they were perfectly formed and white and flawless. But when he picked them up, they broke in half. A terrible and bad-smelling fluid ran out of the white bodies. His father said he could hardly get rid of the odor. If you opened any one of them up, Moultrie thought, that is what they would smell like. Corpses.

They stopped at Moultrie's cell.

"I don't know about this meeting," Spoons said.

"I got to feel him out. I got to see what I'm up against. You do what you can."

"Alright."

5

THE last few days had passed too quickly for Breen; this morning his new assistant was to arrive. He did not sleep well and rose early. Got a cup of coffee and read his office by his bedroom window. It rattled with the wind and he read until daylight. At five thirty, the first-shift guards began to arrive. He watched them through the bars of his window. Many were driven by their wives in cars old and battered. Wives handing over lunch pails and quick morning kisses. The old cars roaring away, blowing leaves and cold dust behind them. One or two guards smoked cigarettes in the long shadows of the guntowers, then stamped them out and entered.

Breen read until he finished his office, then worried some more about the new man and why he was being sent. The Provincial said it was to break him in. Breen wondered. *There's always a catch.* He got up and went to the courtyard and weeded for an hour. He sweated and got his hands good and dirty and felt better. For four days he had not eaten breakfast. Already he thought he could tell the difference in his belly. *It might be nice to have somebody around to talk to.*

Later, back in the kitchen, he looked at his bulletin board and realized that today was Wednesday and the football team practiced early. He had decided last practice that what they needed was a little more running. It would help get out of their systems whatever was eating at them lately. John Carter and Tom Higgins gave him the most trouble. They were doing life and thought they were tough cookies. But he needed big boys and they had sacked the Red quarterback many times. He tried to get as many murderers as he could on the team. They were usually tough and big, but the best natured, easiest to coach.

The first prison game was not played until late October when the heat had eased and the men were not as apt to lose their tempers. Four years he had coached the Blue and lost only three games. This year Red didn't have a real coach. The Methodist chaplain had quit and two or three inmates had taken over. Breen hated to see the Methodist coach go. He loved to beat bad losers, particularly Protestants. He went up to his room, got his gear together, and went out to the playing field, a large rectangle of grass situated in front of the prison, surrounded by the double fences and guntowers.

Practice went well. The block and tackle boys looked good and the extra laps had helped. But during break time, he sensed something strange about the men. The tone of their voices or the way they held their cigarettes, a certain quickness to their eyes—something.

Probably just horny, he thought, and jumped in the shower. In the middle of "Kevin Barry," the hot water began running out. "Well, hell," Breen grumbled, "that's another thing that's got to be fixed." He dried off, put on his habit, and went down to the kitchen, feeling hungry. He took out a plate of ham and cheese. Looking at it for a moment, he sighed and put the plate back. Settled for black coffee and an apple. But there's one damn thing for sure, he told himself, thumping a fist on the table, this kid better not be like the rest of these flunkies who sit around "relating" to one another. Telling their parishioners ways to rationalize sodomy and bilk the government and exhorting young women to yank babies out of their wombs like rabbits out of hats!

He threw the apple core into the sink. Once, by God, once he could have had the whole bunch thrown right out of the Church. In Rome, he had known men, good men. They had the power. The Roman cardinals had liked him because he was big and broad. They used him at their Masses. He had been the youngest American priest to be so honored. In the crowds, he made way for the good men of the Church. He was a soldier. Even then he knew he could not be a holy man, but he hoped to be strong. To sweep the world from the Church's doorstep so that good men, holy men could work. The cardinals had liked him and he thought some one of them would see him bishop. On many feast days, he preached to the Dominicans and the Passionists, even the Carthusians. But all that was a long time ago, and he had lost his temper and everything else. After twenty

41

years, he had learned just to chip away. It was too bad. He would have been good in Rome. But he had learned to live with the brass tacks of God.

The back door buzzer rang. Breen gulped a swallow of coffee. "Must be him." He snorted and tramped to the back door and threw it open.

"Father Breen? I'm White, Michael White."

Slim features, dark, about six feet. They shook hands.

"Wondered when you were coming," Breen said.

"If this place is as hard to get out of as it is to get into, there shouldn't be any problems. Those guys searched my car for half an hour."

"That's their job. Need any help with the bags?"

"Take it easy, Ed. I'll get them myself."

White went down the stairs and brought up the bags easily.

Take it easy, Ed—huh? Breen poured two cups of coffee.

"Pretty grim place," White said, motioning with a thumb toward the door.

"It's a prison," said Breen, shoving a cup of coffee toward him. "Come on. It's your first day, we'll celebrate and sit in the dining room."

The dining room table was oak and big and sat robustly scarred beneath a dusty chandelier and sooty pictures of Thomas Aquinas.

"You'll have to excuse this room. It *is* pretty grim. Maybe me and you, we can paint it sometime? You do know how to paint—a wall?"

"Sure," White said. "Could I have some cream?"

"Cream?" Breen said staring at White, who immediately dropped his eyes. "The milk's in the kitchen."

42

Breen noticed White's hands. The fingers were slim and dark and even the nails perfectly rounded and without flaw. His own hands were rough and full of bristle, with jagged nails. Folded them under the table. *Take it easy, huh?*

White filled his coffee with milk. Breen drank his down straight and banged the mug on the table.

"How do you like that coffee?"

"Pretty good."

"You should make a little noise. Let people know how you feel. That's what all you guys believe in, right?"

"It's real good. Real good coffee," White said, becoming pale.

Breen propped up his feet on a chair. "You know, in seminary, we used to get up, I don't know—five thirty. How about you?"

"About six."

" 'Course ours was a farm, too. We worked before we prayed. Taught us things like—the Bible, Fathers of the Church, for starters. I guess you learned how to organize sit-ins, wet-nurse urban blacks. Crap like that."

"It's still pretty much theology. I just translated a chapter of *Urbs Dei* for a new book coming out."

"Oh, is that so?"

White sipped at his coffee. Watched the big priest roll up the sleeves to his habit. He had never seen arms that big.

"Well, tell me. What kind of new ideas does the eminent young scholar have for running this place?"

"I just thought I would help out with whatever you needed."

"We'll see about that." He looked at White. *I'll be*

damned! He's blushing. Really blushing. "Come on. What ideas have you got? You must have thought about this job a little. What the hell are you going to do here?"

"I don't know. Maybe work with the younger men."

"Oh yes . . . the younger men. I suppose that means guitars and hootenannies in my chapel. Well, let me tell you something, White. There hasn't been a lousy guitar in my chapel yet—and there won't be. And it's a crummy idea! You got that?"

"Yes, Father."

"In fact, it's one of the crummiest ideas I've ever heard, and if you want to work here, you better come up with some better ones than that." Breen was surprised to find himself on his feet. "I'll show you where you sleep!"

He lunged out of the room. Moved more quickly than usual up the stairs. At the top, waited impatiently for White.

"Didn't mean to offend you, Father—I . . ."

"It's not offense I'm worried about, White. Never mind. Here's your room." Breen banged the door with a fist. He gave White a key from his pocket.

White inserted the key and twisted. Nothing happened. He put one leg against the door and pushed. The door would not open.

Breen watched. He said nothing. It bothered him somehow to start giving up these little secrets. There would be the combination of the safe and the wine cellar keys and the little trick with the thermostat. Why should he give them over to a boy who did not even have common sense?

"Pull up and to the right," Breen finally said.

44

At once the door opened.

"You'll share a bath with me. I don't like messes. If you wear cologne, you keep it in your room, bub. I don't want to smell it on my altar or my bath mat."

The room had a bed, chest of drawers, and one chair. There were no curtains.

"We'll talk about your plans for this place later." Breen left him and felt triumphant, though he was somewhat annoyed that White accepted the key and did not offer to give it back. After all, he was superior of this house and he had the right to keep the key himself, and maybe he would.

"White," he yelled, halfway down the stairs.

"Yes?"

"Toss down that key."

"Beg pardon?"

"The key to your room. You throw it down here."

White threw the key down.

"Doors to private rooms are kept unlocked. You need this key, you ask me." Breen turned to go down the steps, then stopped and turned back around. "White?"

"Yes?"

"It's 'Yes, Father.' And say it so I can hear you."

White said it. Louder.

"You pretty good with those lovely hands of yours?"

"Beg pardon?"

"The hot water heater's busted. Fix it!"

45

6

WALSH had not worked a strip-shake before and was sweating hard under the strong lights. "We got to have all those on?"

"We'll need them. Back ten years ago this used to be the main operating room, you know. Yes sir, probably had more guys kick off here than the chair." Langford Cays squinted at the bank of lights. "Lot of guys hate to pass through this place now. At night, they say things move around in here."

"Oh, come on," Walsh said.

"They say one guy—angel of death, they call him— they say he won't take any visitors 'cause he has to go back through this room."

"Who?"

"John Darcy. Niggers call him 'angel of death.' Say

he can walk through walls. Kill anybody he wants. Typical nigger story."

"What about the whores?"

"Thing is—guys really get horny around here. They can even smell a dog in heat, so we take the whores last. If we didn't, these guys would screw them right here, right in front of us." Cays ran a hand through his red hair, hitched his cigar to the other corner of his mouth and screwed down one eye against the smoke. He said that whores were a lot like women. Usually, at the end of the month, they bled a lot and got mean. Because most men didn't screw until the end of the month when they got their pension checks. The whores had to take five or six a night then and "they get tore up pretty bad."

Cays explained the method of searching. The men stripped completely and emptied their pockets on the tables. "You got to run your hands over every seam of clothing, specially underwear." Next the nose, mouth, ears, and soles of the feet had to be searched. "Then comes the fun part. They grab their ankles and you run your finger up their butt, feeling for contraband."

"I get a glove or something, right?"

"You get everything you need," Cays said, smiling. "What you got to watch for is things like handcuff keys taped to the soles of feet. Sometimes, they stick little files up their ass. If they got a bad cut, you check to make sure the stitches are tight, then you feel it for pills. Sometimes they'll cut a pocket in themselves and fill it with pills. You got to watch these things. How do you like it so far?"

"I'll make it," Walsh said.

From under the table just in front of them, Cays pulled

47

out a large jar of Vaseline. "You smear this on your butt finger. Otherwise they yell like hell." Cays grinned at Walsh, then took a boxtop out of his pants pocket and slipped it into an envelope whose address was written in crayon.

"You ever try these things?"

"Letters?"

"Jingle contests. Cereal companies mostly."

"Not really."

"Write them in crayon real wide and clumsy. Makes those dopes think a kid did it. Every year, I pull in forty or fifty prizes."

"Nice," Walsh said, not sure whether he was being put on or not. He set his jaw and waited. The Vaseline was slowly cooking under the hot lights and filling the room with a rancid odor when the first men drifted in from the visiting room. In front of the guards and the long table, they stripped quickly. Held their socks and underwear in one hand, pants, shirt, and shoes in the other.

Walsh's first man was T. J. Rollins. Walsh searched through his pants and shirt. "Open your mouth," he said. Rollins hung his hands from his hips, opened his mouth, and wagged his tongue. Walsh checked his ears and nose with a small flashlight. He looked at the soles of his feet. Then he ran his fingers along the seams of the underwear, which felt sweaty and smelled. He tried not to think about what he was doing. He turned to Cays.

"Okay. I need a glove or something."

The men watching him. Cays threw a large rubber glove. Walsh slipped it on, but the fingers had been cut off.

The men roared and slapped their thighs. Cays was

48

laughing harder than anyone else. "Bottom drawer, there's a box of surgical gloves," he managed to say.

The men were still laughing. Walsh forced himself to laugh, too. Put on one of the gloves. Did not use Vaseline. "Grab your ankles," he said to Rollins. Rollins bent over. A few men whistled. Walsh rammed his finger in hard.

"Sonofabitch!" Rollins yelled.

An hour or so before, Walsh had been standing beneath the smoking shed in the Yard. The rain was drumming against the tin roof and he did not hear Lieutenant Rhiner behind him.

"Why didn't you take the money?"

Walsh jumped, spun around.

"When you first got this job, I thought you were a smart kid."

"What money was that?" Walsh recovered. Fifty dollars was too much for just mailing a prisoner's letter. He had it figured for a setup.

"Stupid move, kid."

Walsh searched Rhiner's face carefully. "I wouldn't want to risk my job for a lousy fifty bucks, would I?"

"Cons don't trust men who aren't on the take. Neither do guards."

Walsh's feet were wet and cold. He rocked on his heels and examined the expression on Rhiner's face. "Who needs trust? We just have to have respect, right?" Waiting.

Rhiner cocked his hat on the back of his head. He had blond hair. About forty-five, with a tight, shrewd face. Propped one foot on a box and spoke quietly and patiently. He said that the prison was full of businessmen.

49

Some were bootleggers, some were pimps, and some made leather purses. There were a lot of things men did here. He said they couldn't do all of these things openly because of the law; guards couldn't live on seventy-five a week. So it was a good deal.

"If you get the right guy, you can make a couple thousand a year just helping him out. You watch out for him. He does the same."

"Keeps leather on your feet, huh?" Walsh said. In his gut he disliked Rhiner and everything he was saying.

"There's rules, too. Like they know we don't want guns in here, so they police their own men and keep them out. We know they got to have knives, so, unless there's big trouble, we let them have a few as long as they don't carry them. If they get caught carrying a shiv, they're fair game. It works out. It's all in the way you figure."

Walsh finished his coffee. "So how do you figure me, Lieutenant?"

Rhiner grinned and stamped some mud from his feet. "Well—I think maybe, just maybe, you'll go a long way, which is just what I planned on. I turned down three other men for you, 'cause I felt somehow we're the same kind of animal. You want to be in that front office and so do I. So you're going to do a real good job. And them that picks good gets picked, remember? And I plan to get picked soon."

Walsh said nothing, but Rhiner's kind of insight made him uneasy.

Rhiner had asked him then if he wanted to work inside for a while. The bastard. He never mentioned the details and Walsh said yes. So now he stood underneath the

50

bright lights watching the last of the "regulars" pick up his clothes and leave.

"You want to take a little break or run the girls on through?" Cays asked.

"Run them through," Walsh said.

Cays opened a small box by the light switches and pushed a button. In a few minutes the whores glided in. Two black, three white. They glanced at Cays, but fastened their eyes on Walsh. He stuck his hands in his pockets and looked at the floor.

Lean and smooth, red toenails flashing, sliding and jiggling, twisting and squirming, they come out of their clothes. The room fills with wicked perfumes and lotions, violets and jonquils, purling over the musty scent of men. Wearing mascara and false eyelashes, rhinestones and lockets, they coo and whisper as they line up before Walsh's side of the table.

"Cays, you want to take a couple of these—guys?"

The whores tittered and minced.

"Sure. Montana, get your sweet ass over here."

A tall man with dark hair went over to Cays. The rest stayed where they were. On Walsh's command one stepped forward.

"Name?" Walsh asked.

"Bonnie Nibbs."

Walsh went through the easiest part of the shakedown. Then he put on a new glove. He looked at Cays. "Maybe you could take a couple more on your side."

"Okay. Line up, ladies."

They did not move. They blinked at Walsh with their wide eyes.

Cays shrugged hopelessly.

51

"Grab your ankles, Nibbs," Walsh snapped.

"Take it easy, honey. I'm sore."

"Yeah, just bend over."

Bonnie Nibbs went down.

Walsh put his finger in slowly.

"Oh, baby," Nibbs whispered.

Walsh wanted to stop right there but did not. Cays finally coaxed two more whores to his side of the table. Afterward, Walsh and Cays washed up.

"Hell of a way to make a living, ain't it?" Cays said.

"What kind of a guy is Rhiner?" Walsh asked, feeling he could let his guard down a little with Cays.

"Good guy. Been here a couple years."

"What he says pretty much the truth?"

"Pretty much."

"Second to Freeman in two years—must be smart."

"Listens good. Listening now to whatever's off balance in this place. Whatever's moving."

Walsh took a brush and scrubbed up to his elbows.

Scrubbing and brisk water. Maine. Fleet schooners, smooth dope. Beach games by the cold sea. Patricia—seedlings and glass seals and salty wisdom. Who raised a different kind of song in his ears. But both of them still had things to get straight in their heads. So he was here now.

Later he stood outside again. The tin roof still drummed with the rain. He felt like stripping off his clothes and standing in the rain for an hour. After a while, Rhiner checked back with him.

"How'd it go?"

"Okay."

"Pretty nasty business, huh?" Rhiner said.

"Beats standing in the rain," said Walsh.

7

MOULTRIE had learned to bake bread in little less than a week. Pouring sweat, stinking, the white men slumped by the ovens and retold their absurd tales and often let their bread burn. But Moultrie studied the dough and the baking, sought out the lesson there and stored it: patience and fire. Once he was able to put molasses and brown sugar into some batter. From somewhere beyond the river, out of the hazy line of green trees, rolled a great fog and rain on that day. Moultrie baked ten loaves and, with Spoons's help, sneaked them out of the kitchen and gave them to his brothers. They sat in their cells and ate sweet bread and drank potato whiskey. They watched the rain rush against the windows, the wind blowing brown leaves into the bars. Before Moultrie returned to his cell, one of the older men shook his hand and then kissed it, eyes flashing tears,

53

saying that he had eaten nothing so good in a long time. And Moultrie was amazed that baking a few loaves of bread could bring out such love from them, for he felt it not only from this one man, but from them all and grew more determined than before to bring down the Muslim who was nothing more than silk and Beethoven, a perfumed cancer that ate up his brothers.

Spoons said he had given the message to the Muslim, but some time had passed and Moultrie worried now. He had heard nothing. He had tried to move first and quick, but the Muslim was taking too much time. Moultrie knew Spoons was afraid. When he walked now, he tried to lift his bad leg higher so the brace would not drag so much, so everyone would not know when he was coming. In the morning, Moultrie finished working early. He went back to his cell and began scrubbing it down. There would be order in his cell. The smallest of his possessions must have its known place, in the night and in the day. This room and these walls were a steppingstone, and he thought that maybe in a hundred years there would be a marker by this prison saying that here was James Moultrie imprisoned.

The mind and the heart, he told himself. They must work together. Malcolm had failed because he could not see the heart. But the heart Moultrie would never betray. Dunking a brush into a pail, he scrubbed the floor. Felt proud of his hands. They worked well and were not soft. Then, there was King who kept his heart in his eyes and so became blind. And Moultrie knew how good and tender that was; but without cunning, a man became helpless. They had shot out King's eyes, his heart, because he loved too much.

54

"Are you Mr. Moultrie?"

Moultrie turned to the bars and knew instantly who his visitor was though he had never before seen him. The Muslim had a closely shaven head and high cheekbones. He was thin. "You must be Mr. Shebrar," Moultrie said, wondering how long the Muslim had been watching him. Angered at being caught off guard.

The Muslim eased in.

"The floor's wet. I was cleaning."

"I'll just stand here. The cell looks very nice," the Muslim said. His eyes were quick. He held himself very straight.

"A little work. I believe in those things," Moultrie said.

"Yes." His accent was a fake Bahamian. He paused, then spoke, measuring his voice. "We have heard of you. Your work with the young has been extraordinary. You are a good speaker."

Moultrie dried his hands and calmed down. This man was a pimp. Moultrie had seen many of them. He was like the rest and Moultrie knew what he should say, but first he wanted to pick him clean.

"I used to do a lot of that. There was a time for it. Were you in any of the marches? Did you see them?"

"I have seen them." The Muslim smiled a little smile. "Those were strong moves. They let the white man know."

Moultrie leaned against the wall, then saw something under the Muslim's left eye that chilled him—a small, blue tattooed snake. "What did you do to let the white man know?"

The Muslim gave a slow grin. His work shirt pocket

55

stuffed with a red silk handkerchief. "Your friend, Mr. Spoons, said we might discuss a little business."

Casually, Moultrie wiped at his face and hung a hand from his belt. "You know, I worked with some good men. They taught me a lot. There was really something to them. One thing they never did, though. They never sold out their people. Never tried to make a buck off of them. That's really something, huh?"

The blue snake twitched with the Muslim's eyes. "The whites are our trouble. They are bright wolves, but they will fade."

"That's one thing I just don't believe in. Letting things fade out. Sometimes you got to stomp on things a little. Cut off the offending hand. You know what I mean?"

"Yes." The Muslim's eyes narrowed.

Moultrie rubbed his hands across his pants. "My daddy used to have some goats when I was a child. Beautiful things. Black as Lazarus' tomb. He paid a lot of money for them, but for some reason they just didn't do well, you know? Man, they got skinnier and skinnier. They finally died. We found out it was leeches. Swamp leeches. We could have got rid of them, but they were black. We just couldn't see them. They could suck right on those goats' hearts and you could never see them." A quick movement outside the cell brought Moultrie's attention to two shadows. Waiting.

The Muslim caught his eyes. "Mr. Moultrie, I must be going. I work in the sign shop and there are many to be done today. You are a very attractive young man. You speak well. You must watch out for yourself here. Some- times—it is very dangerous."

Moultrie slid up close to him. "Let me tell you some-

56

thing, Muslim. You don't scare me and neither do your niggers out there. You better think about what I said today. I've brought down bigger men than you."

The Muslim eased by Moultrie out of the cell. He turned to stand and look at him, then, his face cold and hard, disappeared into the dark.

Sonofabitch, Moultrie thought. He felt elated. Outside, he ran into pushers, pimps, twice that tough. The Muslim was a weak little man. Moultrie was not afraid of such men. They had to learn respect for you. They had to see that you could get tough, too. He felt confident and excited. He looked out his cell door. The tier was empty. He turned back around and lay down on his bed and pulled the wool blanket over him, slipping away from this place.

Remembering the great deer blanket his father wrapped him in as a boy, dark and soft, covered in the red, lost-eyed, prancing deer. On clear winter nights when the sharp wind tried to make kindling out of the house, his father called out, "You warm, boy?" "Yes, sir," the boy said. Then there was a silence that they both understood, and his father came into the room on bare feet. "Better wrap up in this. It's colder than a brier patch." His father turned his head and listened toward the dark. The wind, in compliance, tore through the black chinaberry trees. "Yes, sir. You put this ole blanket 'round you, son."

And the boy did. Then the boy said that the air was too cold in his room and it hurt his throat like outside. This was a joke between them, for he was a very small boy then and both of them liked these games.

His father went into the next room, which was dark

57

except for the wood fire. The boy could see him from his room. His father blew up two or three balloons and held them close to the flames. He came back into the boy's room and tucked him in good. His hands seemed brave and splendid and big as the world. The boy could smell a little whiskey and sweat from him. His father held the balloons just above his heart and let the warm air rush out across the boy's face. It was green sourwood and he went fast asleep, dreaming of soft darkness and deer and good fires.

Someone was shaking him by the shoulder. He started, then saw Spoons.

"You shouldn't depend on the tier boy, man. You should have your own lock, too. How'd it go?"

Moultrie sat on the edge of the bed, rubbing his eyes. "That bastard's a piece of cake."

"Did you talk business to him? Did you get yourself a little insurance?"

"He's not worth the trouble. We get to his boys, he'll be out in a week."

"Moultrie, you talked business, right? You made it sound like a deal?"

"I can eat guys like that for breakfast. Don't you remember that guy in D.C. . . . ?"

"This ain't D.C., man. This ain't nothing like D.C. Don't you see that?"

Moultrie ran some water in the basin, splashed his face. "You calling the shots now?"

"He could have your throat slit in five minutes, if he wanted to."

Moultrie grabbed Spoons by the collar. "What the hell's the matter with you? You've let this place get to

58

you, man. I can think circles around that guy. And no-body, nobody slits my throat!" Letting loose of him, Moultrie quickly glanced outside the door. He kicked his suitcase under the bed.

Spoons lit a cigarette. Adjusted his brace.

"You gotten to those guys yet?" Moultrie asked.

"A guy in whiskey and one in dope. They're nervous. It'll take some doing."

"They're nervous, huh? The Muslim, I bet he's nervous, too. He should be. Right now, he's on his way down," Moultrie said. He stared out toward the tiers, a fire streaming through his veins. "We sucker these guys along, Spoons. We make them think we're one of them. Then when the Muslim's out, we wreck this show, this corruption."

"How?"

"We're just going to do it!"

8

Maybe the water has some secret in it. Maybe its secret will mix with the dark liquid and there will be a miracle.

"What's that god-awful smell?" John Hawkins asked from the cell door. He was short and thin with dark eyes and hair.

"What smell?"

"Smells like a burning skunk or something."

Childs glanced in the mirror.

"It's coming from that bottle. What is that crap?"

"It's nothing," Childs said, blushing, putting the bottle away.

"Come on, Childs. What is that stuff?"

Childs worked his hands in his pockets. "In two weeks it makes your beard grow. I saved the guarantee." He pulled out the guarantee and showed it to John Hawkins, who laughed. Childs did not laugh and Hawkins stopped.

"Why are you doing that?"

"I like to shave, too. Lookie here." Childs took a shaving mug and brush from his dresser. "It was my granddaddy's. He gave it to me and I want to use it. I know that stuff will work. They sent me the guarantee. Two weeks."

Hawkins looked at him and shook his head.

"You're crazy." They walked down the tier toward the snack bar.

"Do they still whistle?" Hawkins asked.

"Not so much now. Why do they do that?"

"Why the hell do you think? Because you're ugly, Childs. They whistle at ugly people."

Childs had not known John Hawkins long and did not understand everything he said or meant. But he liked Hawkins right off because he was raised in a mill town too, and they could talk easy and trade stories. Hawkins came from a family of weavers, and he was proud of it. Weaving was a good, hard trade. Not like carding. Childs's father was a carder, which usually meant a sober drunk—sometimes—during work and a drunk drunk after. But Hawkins did not seem ashamed to hang around him, even when he said stupid things. Childs knew he did that often, but he also knew that he was blessed. He was the gift. He was the miracle. His mother had told him that he had been healed at the revival when he was six— when he stood up and walked for the first time, and all the doctor's dark promises fell away. Not long afterward he was given his prayer language, and he could talk secretly to the Lord. Though to this day he was not quite sure of what the Lord was, he thought of him as three

61

things: maker, taker, and the burning bush. And when he knelt down and began his prayers, the strange words filled his heart with little lights which glowed in him like lightning bugs and made him feel good.

The snack bar was made out of a converted cell. It held cold drinks, sandwiches, cookies, stacks of cigarettes, a few packages of snuff, tobacco. Next to the drink cooler sat a box of cheese and sardines. Onions steeped in a big fish bowl. The odor cut hard through the dark air. The onions cost a dime each and were usually saved for movies or football games. Hawkins and Childs looked for a while, then decided on cereal. They paid, emptied the cornflakes into plastic bowls, and took their milk and sat down by the churning washing machines at the far end of the building.

"They appealing your case?"

"Don't have the money."

"Five good years."

"I didn't do it."

"Uh-huh."

"My friends just said we was going for a ride. I didn't know nothing about them holding up the store till the policemen stopped us."

Hawkins rolled his eyes. "And your friends. Where are they now?"

Childs didn't know and felt bad, for he was telling the truth.

"You got a lot of work today?" Hawkins asked.

"There's a lot of trucks on Monday, usually."

"You should get a new job."

"It's not too bad except for fruit. The bees get you with fruit."

"Too bad. I think they had grapes last night "

"It'll be bad," Childs said.

Hawkins told one of his nice stories then. About the night he got his first piece. He was thirteen and pitching on the Olympia mill team against Fairview, back when Fairview mills never got beat more than once a season. Hot, August night and the beetles whined and clashed under the lights and the stands were crammed with first and second shifts from both mills and the air smelled rotten, almost made his eyes burn from the new dyeing process going on at Olympia, just across the street. Hawkins said he knew he had the stuff in him that night when he was taping up, and sure enough on the mound he fanned their asses, pitched the shutout. The best fight came then when the stands blew up and third shift from Olympia came running over, wheeling bobbins and whipping ass in the red dust and the blood and the beer. Somehow though, Hawkins said, he got left behind when Fairview got chased out of town. But that was alright because he snagged the little cheerleader who was watching him all night, and in the dugout, on a long, gritty bench, did it the first time. Not bothering to take off his tape or cleats, and she was sixteen and tight bellied and shook her pompon through it all.

Childs wanted to follow up with a good story too, but he couldn't talk like Hawkins. He sat quietly for a while then asked something that was worrying him. "How much money we need a month here?"

"Forty, fifty bucks a month covers trash," Hawkins said.

Trash was extra soap or towels, snacks, newspapers—all very expensive here. Childs felt a little frightened. It

63

was alright for Hawkins. He made ninety cents an hour in the laundry and got to work six hours a day. But Childs only worked two hours a day at most, and his parents couldn't send much if any money. Besides that, all money made in prison was paid out to you in plastic chips, and the vendors always charged more when you paid them in plastic money. But the smart guys like the Hawk made enough every week to pay out some of their money to guards or trusties and get plastic changed to silver. Trash was cheaper for them.

Hawkins finished his cereal first. "How about taking my bowl back for me? I got to get to work."

"Alright," Childs said.

"You watch out for them bees."

"I will." Childs finished his cereal and put the bowls on the canteen counter. He decided to go back to his cell and sew until the whistle blew for him.

For a change, he climbed the back stairwell. On the platform to the third tier stood eight or nine men, but he decided there was enough room for him to pass. When he got to the third platform, they had all spread out. They stared at him. They were sifting change in their pockets and tugging cigarettes. Polishing their red hands like apples against their jeans.

Childs turned to go back, but two of them had slipped behind him. A man with a sharp, red face stepped out of the crowd.

"Well, lookie here what done wandered up to ole R. L., boys. Why, ain't it the prettiest pussy boy you ever saw?"

He ran his hand through Childs's hair.

Childs slapped the hand away. "Let me alone," he said.

64

"Whew—she's a feisty one," R. L. Atkins said, blowing on his hand. He turned to the others. "Now, how'd you boys like to have this little thing in your sack at night to keep the rheumatism away?"

The men were hollering and hooting.

"You leave me alone," Childs said.

"Don't you worry, sugar. We ain't going to hurt you. I just want to show my buddies something." He stuck his face in Childs's. "They's good ole boys."

Two men grabbed Childs from behind. Doubled him over a handrail and pinned his arms. His head dangled over the cement floor three stories down. R. L. Atkins unbuckled Childs's trousers and let them fall. He smoothed a hand over Childs's butt.

"Bastard! You bastard!" Childs tried to yell, but he was choking.

"Gag him," Atkins said.

Someone rammed a handkerchief into Childs's mouth. The men packed in as close as they could.

Feels someone's hand—cold, sliding over him, pinching, calluses on the palms, raking him. Afraid, waiting for something worse, feeling himself shiver. Gagging on the handkerchief, trying not to cry, not to vomit. Waiting.

"Now, there's a night mama there, boys!"

Not hearing them laugh this time, a different sound— hissing, quick, high breaths, then many hands on him, many fingers prodding, shooting up between his legs. Hurting, caressing, tugging at him and he tries to break free, arms numb, knowing he will vomit now, tears stinging his eyes. Then, at once, the hands are gone.

R. L. Atkins pushed the others back. "This is the way she'll go." Mocking rape, he laced his fingers over his zipper leaving a small hole. Slowly he began to swivel his

65

hips. Pawed the ground with his feet and circled around and around—growling, squalling in his throat like a bobcat. Then he dived straight into Childs, humping faster and faster, hooting and squawking while the men squirmed and strained to get closer.

Down below a whistle was blowing and two guards raced up the stairs. The men quickly let Childs go and started running down the tier. Someone snatched the handkerchief out of his mouth, and he tried to grab him but missed. He lay on the platform trying to make his arms work, trying not to get sick. He was buckling his pants just as the guards got to him.

"What the hell's going on up here?" one guard asked.

Childs swallowed, rubbed his arms. "Those boys . . . those boys were teasing me. They pulled down my britches."

One of the guards looked at the other, then he looked at Childs again. "Okay. What happened?"

"I told you. They was teasing me and they pulled down my pants and I think they were going to give me the red-butt."

"Give you the what?"

"The red-butt."

The guards laughed.

"Aren't you going to get after them?"

"Ain't you new here?"

"Yes, sir."

"Well, maybe you just better watch where you go around this place." The guards went back down the stairs, still laughing.

He went up to his cell and took out his sewing. Once in a while, he thought he heard someone talking outside

66

his door, but when he looked, no one was there. He wouldn't go up the back stairs anymore. It was too dark and the men had meant something else besides the redbutt. He felt something from them, from all the men here. That they sensed him even when they could not see him, like roaches. Scuttling back and forth in their cells, wearing long antennae from their heads which smelled him out, swished after him even in the dark. He would not go up the back stairs again.

9

A sharp turn and Walsh leaned into the door, while the truck whined along the dirt road. Past the brown and gray autumn fields, riding with Rhiner toward the prison farm, which lay a good ten miles into the scrub-oak countryside. Suddenly the truck lurched with a loud pop and sank low on the right. Rhiner swerved toward a ditch, made a good save.

"Blow out," Rhiner snorted.

The prisoners grumbled in the back.

Rhiner handed Walsh a key. "Let them out and watch their asses." He nodded toward the shotgun clamped against the dashboard. "Take it. Let them know you'll use it."

Walsh kept his mouth shut around Rhiner. He didn't like the things the lieutenant said or the way he put them.

He threw open the back doors of the truck and four men came blinking out into the sunlight, the clean-smelling woodlands. Somehow the gun felt good in his hands and this bothered him. He had not picked one up since the last time he hunted with his father. Since he was seventeen and could pop the eyes out of a squirrel at sixty yards. But guns were for killing and he was not, and it bothered him that the stock felt good in his hands.

Rhiner supervised the tire change, speaking direct and cold to two of the men.

"Could I bum a match, man?"

Walsh cautiously held the shotgun in his left hand. The prisoner seemed not much older than himself, but had a hard white face and curious, pointed eyes. "Sorry, don't smoke."

"Me neither, till I got blowed into this place."

"What you in for?" Walsh asked and felt the prisoner's eyes stitching up and down his face. Studying him.

"Whores used to give you free matches with a lay sometimes. Not anymore though. They're all wrecked, man. Some new dude's got guys ready to fight over him. Some real bad asses, too. My name's Peterson," he said, abruptly smiling and sticking out his hand.

Walsh gripped it, soul style. Noticing the three or four bright butterfly tattoos.

"How'd you end up being a screw?"

"Just making a little bread."

"Child molesting," Peterson said quickly, looking carefully about him. "Bum rap. Never touched him. Bum deal, man. But you could give me a hand."

"How's that?" Walsh asked, startled by Peterson's confession.

69

"I used to be out here. Out at the farm. But I got in some trouble, see? A little dope. Nothing big. But they put me back behind the walls. Those guys back there— the cons—they're judge and jury all over again. If they think you're a—pervert, you're dead."

"Don't give me that."

"You could put in a request to have me moved back out here. Come on. Give me a break."

"Alright, haul it in," Rhiner yelled, moving toward Walsh.

Peterson was backing into the truck. "Think about it. All you got to do is ask, man. That's all."

Rhiner slammed the doors behind the men, padlocked it.

They had been riding along for a while, Walsh turning over Peterson's plea, when Rhiner said that the prison felt like a skillet and it was good to get out. Walsh recounted Cays's uneasiness and Rhiner gave his head a little jerk, clucked his tongue.

"We wait it out. Count the silverware. When they start hoarding spoons, then we worry."

Just inside the farm's simple gate, Rhiner turned down a side road. He said that this was a special day and when Walsh asked why, Rhiner said just to wait. It was a little education for him. Pulling the truck over, he gave Walsh some netting and told him to let the men out. They knew what to do.

Walsh was leaning against the truck, pulling the netting tighter about his face. Not yet daring to take his hands from his pockets. Watching the puffs of smoke fill the air. Now smelling the sharp ashes.

Rhiner lifted up his netting, sliding on a pair of sunglasses. Pointed to a maple tree. "Those're starlings, I think. Yep, starlings. They'll fly to another tree—closer to the action." Rhiner was craning his neck, searching the area. "That cedar, I bet. This place has ruined them. The comb. They expect too much."

Suddenly, with a loud screaming, the birds burst from the maple, riddling the cedar. Rhiner turned halfway to Walsh, smiling.

The droning was becoming stronger now, moving down with the east wind.

Carefully watching his hands, Walsh drew out a new plug of tobacco from his back pocket. Tugged a bit free, packing it into his jaw with his tongue. As yet, he still couldn't spit too well, but each day he improved. At least it did not sting his mouth so much now.

The prisoners began fanning out behind the long lines of hives, squeezing their smokers, circling a large, rotted oak.

"Hold this," Rhiner said, handing Walsh a shotgun. "They're prone to light out through the woods if they don't see a little gauge."

Walsh held the shotgun in the crook of his arm, enjoying the fresh wind and sun of the farm. Waiting.

Out of a decaying shack on the edge of the woods, a white-haired black man emerged. Standing in front of one of the hives, he began stripping away his shirt, trousers.

"What's going on?" Walsh asked, bewildered. Rhiner did not answer.

Naked now in the warm autumn sun, the beekeeper's skin flashed with freshly painted symbols—red, blue, and green, to keep him from being stung, Rhiner said. He

71

lifted the top off a hive, drawing out a long, narrow slat of honey.

The starlings were screaming, scolding in the cedar tree as the old man gently, gracefully, as if clearing water to drink, herded the bees from the honey, back into the hive. Under the pale sun, the golden comb gave in to the pressure of the beekeeper's hands. Pouring down his arms, oozing through his dry fingers, as he smeared it over his body.

"Jesus Christ!" Walsh said. "They'll kill him."

"Not in twenty-five years they haven't," Rhiner said, watching the old man as he approached the rotted oak.

With a wide, slow extension of his arms, the beekeeper motioned the prisoners away from the tree.

Walsh held the shotgun tightly across his chest, as the starlings swept down from the cedar tree and devoured the broken, gleaming comb.

A dark, rumbling sound bellowed from the oak as the beekeeper struck it with a limb. With the rumbling, the starlings became quiet.

Like a black wraith caught in the sunlight, the bee-keeper extended his long, cracked hands toward the tree and, mimelike, gracefully settled them back upon his chest. And as they alighted for the last time, he uttered a sound, a cry, deep inside his hollow ribs, his head softly lolling from side to side.

"Lieutenant, what the hell's . . . ?" Walsh was saying until he heard it, like an echo, something deep, mournful within the oak.

Walsh could see the beekeeper smile.

Like a tendril of ink, like a trickle of night flowing into the pale sky, poured the wild bees, gradually losing

72

their resonance until only a hiss was left to the oak, and that, too, finally gone.

Though they fell on him hard and at once, the beekeeper did not flinch. Slowly, he turned and approached one of the empty hives.

From the prisoners standing just behind the hives came a sudden noise, a sharp crackling of branches. Rhiner quickly signaled them to be still.

A human form, arrayed in wild, now softly murmuring bees, moving toward an empty hive. And cautiously, by gentle motions, the beekeeper was coaxing them from his body. Taking a rack of comb from the new hive, dabbing a bit of honey into its cells. Then, as if by a spell, the bees began setting him free, burying themselves like dark bullets into the comb.

Again from the prisoners came a quick, sudden movement, a noise.

"Level that gauge on those men," Rhiner whispered.

Walsh looked at him.

"Level it, goddammit!"

Feeling the smooth stock against his chin, seeing the surprised, now very still faces between the barrels.

The beekeeper now on his knees, his head laid across his arms on the step of the hive.

"Something's wrong," Rhiner said, ripping off his veil. "Keep those guys still." He took a smoker, carefully moving toward the old man, squeezing the bellows.

The air smelled of honey and ash. The beekeeper seemed all motion, brimming with the soft, glittering honey and the dark bees, wild of the woods, yet he did not move when Rhiner whispered his name. Gradually, there seemed some kind of filling, spreading. Walsh

73

flicked his eyes back between the barrels. When he looked again, there seemed to be more bees, as if they had somehow increased, making the beekeeper's body larger, out of proportion. Rhiner was calling out his name, louder now. Silence, except for a droning, like from the oak, but shallower.

Walsh let his gun down. Rhiner's smoker was wheezing frantically in the silence, then ceased and fell to the ground, as the bees began swarming toward the old man's head. High against the sun they collected, murmuring like a darker wind, and then were gone. Deep into the bare forests, sharply through the clean, smooth trees, swiftly above the fast arrowhead creeks.

Swelling and naked, the beekeeper slumped against the earth. Shimmering in honey, while the failing smoker reeled its last ashy breath, while the starlings pitched and screamed in the trees above the broken comb.

"Let them have it," Rhiner said, pointed toward the starlings. "Shut them the hell up!"

The shotgun echoed through the barren countryside.

Back in the truck, riding toward the prison dairy: sweat, the soft, polluted river mud steaming from the prisoners' boots, the buckets of honey, sweet and heavy. Hearing the talk about the beekeeper's death, that it was a bad omen, very bad, and that something would come of it. Wait and see. Walsh wondered if Rhiner felt anything. If there was any sensitivity at all to him. A man he had known, or at least seen for some years, had just died. Stung to death, for God's sake, and his body still swelling in the back of the truck. For one moment he almost let himself go. Almost grabbed Rhiner by the neck and told him he stunk. Then somehow his anger and Peterson's

74

plea and the beekeeper's death caught him in the belly. He turned his head and vomited out the window.

Rhiner said nothing.

When they arrived at the dairy, the men began loading milk. Walsh exchanged a glance with Peterson, then moved out among the farm buildings, the sweet smell of manure and grain. He felt relieved to be away from Rhiner. From such disregard of life and spirit. Perhaps it came from being at the main prison. Too many men. Too much stone and mortar. Here the prisoners seemed calm, red-cheeked. Guntowers rose against the sky, but somehow were less threatening, softer above the stand of pines that clustered about their base. Even the guards seemed loose-jointed and easy, not bothering to cover their backs by standing close to a wall.

If there had to be prisons they should be like this one. Rural, healthy. Allowing men to work, to pride themselves from work.

When he returned he found a smaller truck parked beside the other. Inside lay the beekeeper's body surrounded with buckets of honey and cool cisterns of milk and the spent smokers of ash. It was a good, honorable way for him to be carried. The prisoners or maybe even the guards of the farm looked after their own.

Rhiner brushed by him, shining the bill of his hat with his sleeve. "Think we'll get sausage for lunch?"

10

"S O M E of those guys must kill a quart a day," White said.

"Depends on how good it is," said Breen, annoyed that White was interrupting the football game.

"They'll kill themselves doing that."

"That's right," Breen said wearily. He had been up since 3 A.M., since he had given the last rites to Timmy Potter and watched his face gutter, smolder to gray. Alcoholics dying and nothing could be said or done but to hold their cold hands and see them through it. Feeling the poison sucking handfuls of light from their eyes, still feeling the weakness in his own body.

About one hundred alcoholics lived in the prison, drinking their stomachs and eyes out with bad whiskey. Breen had tried hard with all of them his first year. But he knew that some men simply would not live. So he came by two or three days a week now, seeing those who would see him. Played cards or joked with them. Got them what they needed. Two or three men even took a drink in front of him now. He said nothing. Knew it was no use. God loved them more than he could know, so he left it with Him. Prayed for them at Mass. Chipped away.

White had worked out a plan for visiting men in their cells. He ran into some of the alcoholics. At night, in the recreation room, he was talking to Breen about them.

"Don't you care about these men, Father?" White said, abruptly jumping up in front of the television set.

"Sit down, White!"

"Baltimore's going to lose this one by two touchdowns," White said, dropping back into his chair. The game was in the first quarter.

"On a good day, White, on a good day the Blue team could stay right in there with those guys."

White sighed, trying to hold back his temper, cracked his knuckles. "If you ask me, we have to do something about these things. They all add up. Like that old beekeeper dying a couple days ago. Some blacks are really upset about that. Say it means something's about to happen. We ought to talk to them about it. Calm them down. There *is* something in the air. Something brooding. I can feel it."

"Yeah, well, I been here a long time, buddy boy, and I don't feel anything." Breen glared at the television set.

"I have a plan for the alcoholics."

"Give me those peanuts."

"I think it could really work." White handed him the jar.

77

Breen sat back in his chair and rolled up the sleeves of his habit, popping peanuts into his mouth.

"These men need help," White said.

"That's what we have God for, Father."

"Look here, Breen. Just because you get kicked out of the Vatican doesn't mean you go sour on the world!"

Breen jumped out of the chair, slammed an end table into the wall. He pointed a finger in White's face. "You got a big mouth, sonny. A real big mouth. And if you open it up once more like that—I swear to God I'll bust it off for you!"

White looked away. Jammed his hands into his pockets.

Breen was grinding his fist into his hand, waiting for the other man to make a move. Finally, he turned and snapped off the television. Cooled down a bit and turned back to White.

"Let me tell you something, bub. I've been here eight goddamn years. I made some pretty good friends out of drunks. And when they died, I missed the hell out of some of them. But there's nothing you can do. Not a damn thing. If they want to die, they die, and I'm sorry. I pray to God for their souls, but there's nothing I can do. Oh, but I know what you want to do. Start a program, right? Make them believe they can beat the booze, or the drugs, or whatever else is wrong with them. Well, you're dead wrong, buddy, because they can't beat any of it. And after you've made them feel real good, given them hope, and they fall again and think they're nothing but dirt—hurt twice as much as before—then you'll leave it to guys like me and say—well, we had to try, didn't we? Bullshit!" Breen moved to a bookcase. Opened a package of fishfood and dumped half of it into an aquarium. He sat back down.

"It's kind of like a buddy system," White said quietly. "You put two guys in a cell. One an alcoholic, one an AA member. The AA guy talks to, preaches to, watches the other one. He'll be there in the night. There'll be somebody to care."

"It stinks. It won't work," Breen said.

"Why?"

"Where are you going to find all these AA guys?"

"We got thirty or forty in this prison."

"The Warden won't approve it. Too much moving around."

"We'll ask him. We've got to wade into this thing."

"Alright, I'll tell you what. You go ahead. You try this smart-assed idea. You'll get everybody pissed off. Just don't get me involved, okay?"

"Sure," White said. "One more thing. There's a new guy here—P. G. Carter. Wants to see you, get on the team."

"Junkie. I checked him out."

"Okay," White said, clicking on the television. Second quarter and Baltimore was down by one.

The next few days were hard. Two nights in a row Breen was called to the infirmary. His days were spent counseling, listening to complaints, saying Mass. It had been twenty years since he had seen Brazil, just after they had sent him away from Rome. . . . *Just after he had told the head of the Order, Bishop Shehan, right in front of the Sistine Chapel, that he was a fool and that the whole Franciscan Order was playing a game for fools, pretending to embrace poverty when they did not. When*

79

*their bellies and friaries and chapels bulged with the fat-
ness of the world. Sure they owned nothing, but they had
use of everything and had lost the grain of poverty, scattered it beneath their thirty-dollar sandals and their
two-hundred-dollar homespun habits. . . .* It would be
good to hike through those deep forests again. Where
there were no bars, no locked doors. Where the people
said, "Yes, Father" and "No, Father" and knew their
own natures. Did not make confessional promises they
could not keep. Today, he took a couple of hours off.
Slept a while, then went outside.

The prison gym was located just beside the rectory.
Breen had a private door and key. The day was bright
and blue. He had moved the weights out of the gym and
set them in the courtyard. Wore black pants and a sleeve-
less sweat shirt and old tennis shoes. With a bar whistling
the reps out. Feeling his arms stove up. Blowing like a
whale.

On Tuesday night, about eleven o'clock, Breen had
heard a strange sound and gotten up to check. It was
White. He was practicing alternate breathing. Buddhism
was a pile of crap and so was yoga. White should see
that, he thought. He asked about it the next morning and
White said that yoga helped him to relax and that they
taught it at the seminary. He said that once Thomas
Merton came and lectured and after that even the rector
practiced yoga.

Breen started some more curls. Got to pump these
out. He did six and went for eight. At the end, he blew
hard and snorted, "Merton—that creep!" He set the bar
down. "A crackpot from the first day—a Trappist, thank
God!"

80

He wiped his face with a towel and shadowboxed a while. Still got the good jab, he told himself. The Warden had approved part of White's plan. It was a stupid idea. Breen knew it would not work.

Father White strolled outside the rectory, carrying some cloth and needles and thread.

Breen was pretending he did not see him.

"Afternoon," White said.

"Oh—hi. Didn't see you." Breen continued his curls.

"Those guys look pretty serious up there," White said, looking at a guntower.

"They're supposed to be. Thought you had an appointment with the Warden?"

"Postponed it." White sat down on the rectory stairs and began to sew.

Breen watched him a moment. "God Almighty," he mumbled. Slapped twenty pounds more on the bar and tried to do ten reps. He could do only six and felt dizzy. "What you up to?" he asked, coming over to White.

"Making a few banners for the Chapel. Saw you boxing. You have a good left."

"Not bad. Let's have a look at what you're doing."

The banner was green and red. It said: "We Give to You As You Gave to Us."

"Hey, that isn't too bad," Breen said with a big smile. "You been sewing long?"

"Used to do it as a kid. You must have boxed a lot."

"Couple semipro fights. Nothing much. You're going to hang those in the chapel, huh?"

"Not if you don't want me to, Father." White looked at him.

"No, no. Go ahead. I just thought it looked kind of

81

nice the way it was—monastic. But you go ahead. I don't know how to sew."

White put the sewing down. "How much you got on the bar?"

"Gee, I don't know. About a hundred and thirty, I guess. Haven't really been counting."

"Mind if I give it a try?"

"Sure. Go ahead."

White went over and picked up the bar. His face reddened.

"Better take it easy, maybe," Breen said.

White tried a curl. He couldn't move the bar past his belt buckle.

"Yeah, well, you got to work into these things," Breen said, feeling good.

White moved a bench from the outside wall of the gym and placed dumbbells at each end to steady it. Then he stood back, took a deep breath, and jumped onto the bench in a handstand. He walked the length of the bench twice. At the very end, he pivoted away and landed exactly on his feet.

Breen ground his teeth.

"Used to do it blowing 'Dixie' through a Jew's harp, once," White said, barely out of breath.

Breen was doing a few nonchalant deep-knee bends. "Never did too much of that myself. Wasn't built for it."

"Too big, huh?" White said.

"Yeah."

"But you had a couple pro fights, right?"

"Well, semipro, yeah. Did a little of that."

"I was on the sem's boxing team. First man."

"No kidding. You pretty good?"

"Alright. Not the best, but alright."

82

Breen was rubbing a towel at the back of his neck, kicking the ground like a pitcher. White hanging his hands from his hips, folding them under his arms, then hanging them from his hips again.

"Well, I'm going to that inmate meeting. Some kind of grievances."

"Never mind about that crap. That hot water heater's still acting up. So fix it. I'm tired of getting ice in the middle of my showers."

White went over to his sewing. "Oh, one other thing, Father. I thought maybe . . . this is just an idea . . . but maybe we could change our diet a little?"

"What?"

"We eat pretty good here. I don't know, somehow it doesn't seem quite right."

Breen tucked his hands into his back pockets and leaned forward. "I'll tell you what. You go ahead and worry about your waistline, pretty boy. Meanwhile, someone's got to have enough strength to do the work of the Church!"

"Sorry, Father. It was just an idea," White said, retreating with his sewing toward the rectory.

"Yeah. Another crummy, half-assed idea! Why don't you stop thinking up crummy ideas and fix the crummy hot water heater! How about that?"

"Yes, Father. It'll get done, Father," White said and disappeared into the rectory.

"Jesus!" Breen said, throwing the towel to the ground. He stood for a moment, then picked the towel up and went inside the gym. *First man. Shit! Just one punch, a right hander, too. Forget the left. A right hander and that kid'd go down like the* Titanic!

Late that night, he tried to do handstands until two

o'clock in the morning. Once, when he fell, he thought he heard White laugh. He went to bed, but did not sleep well.

In the killing zone, the dogs were howling all night long.

II

What I don't like—and I can take a lot of Moultrie's
bullshit, 'cause I've known him a long time—but what
gets to me, man, is him saying I'm a coward, chicken
shit. Okay, so maybe I do lock myself up in the afternoons—to take a nap. And being in our positions, when
you sleep around here you damn well better have your
door locked. See—Moultrie, Moultrie thinks bucking the
Muslim is some kind of a college sit-in. Some kind of
game. And I'm telling you, if he keeps it up, he's dead.
I know Shebrar. He'll cut his guts out. And like, I can
advise all I want, but if Moultrie doesn't see that—it's all
over. Another thing. I was with him when he talked to
Rayfield Jones—whiskey. Oh, Moultrie's got a way with
people all right. Always has. And he does just fine till
you start talking business, then—oh, shit! It's like he's—

I don't know. It's like he's twelve years old again or something. Like he's talking to that old man of his he brags on so much. Nothing worse than a drunk mortician. Hell, if we're going to pull this thing off, he's got to let these people know he can set the fire and put it out, too. I don't know. Maybe Rayfield Jones will come around. I don't know. But I told Moultrie—and he got pissed off as hell when I did—but I said, you got to be tough with these guys and bluff their ass into the wall. You got to convince them that *you* can get rid of the Muslim and *you* can make them more money and nobody else can do it but you. I put it straight to him, man. Now, the time's good. These guys feel like they're getting ripped off by the Muslim, and maybe they are. Who cares? But Moultrie, goddammit, Moultrie's got to let them know he's their man. Now he's got this meeting with Beauchampes today, and he's the tough one. But I'll tell you what—if we get Beauchampes behind us, if we get dope on our side, then we're home free. That is, if Moultrie remembers to stay out of dark corners and locks his damned cell door. Otherwise, he's one dead nigger! Oh, yeah. One more thing. Moultrie says this whole thing is just a trick to get the Muslim out so he can "save" his brothers from dope and liquor. I don't know if that's true or not. But if he really thinks he can stop men from getting a little pleasure in this pit, he's crazy. If he gets the Muslim out, he should just take over. We got to have order here. We got troubles enough with honky guards who can't decide who's the head honcho. Makes me nervous, man. Makes me real nervous.

* * *

86

"Why the cafeteria?" Moultrie asked.

"Two reasons," Spoons said. "One—lots of light. Two —lots of witnesses. An audience will keep these guys honest."

The tiers of Building One were dark and quiet as they descended to the first floor.

"Maybe it's too open, though. Maybe it'll all get back to him."

Moultrie stopped and smiled at Spoons. "Oh, he's going to find out, man. Maybe he already knows. We've got to beat the Muslim to the punch. That's all. That's the way this game works, or have you forgotten all that in here?"

"I haven't forgotten," Spoons said.

A crowd was gathering at the main gate of Building One.

"I wonder what the hell's wrong. We can't be late for this one," Spoons said.

Moultrie cautiously pressed into the silent group of men. He could see nothing. But faintly, vaguely from the air or from those about him, he sensed something familiar, an odor, a feeling . . . the long Sunday afternoons when he and his brothers would wake up from sticky naps and put their church clothes back on, incredibly sharp and scratchy. Still swollen with chicken and sleep, they slipped by their father's embalming room in the attic and came down to the parlor, their necks damp as wrung rags. It seemed that there was always a great thunderhead swelling up somewhere across the meadow and that the dark parlor was charged and damp. How they sat and waited for company, the house silent and smelling of chicken and death from the attic, while some-

87

where just beyond the trees, the storm was brewing and blowing damp ash through the chimney, drifting down the grate.

"Death," Moultrie said.

"What?"

"Up there. Somebody's died."

"Hell, Moultrie. You can't see any better than I can." Spoons made his way toward the gate. In a few minutes, two men shuffled out with a litter, a body. Spoons followed. Looked at Moultrie strangely. "Sam Guest. Heart attack."

Two doors for the cafeteria, two lines of men. Guards patrolling.

Moultrie's plate was passed down ahead of him. He had no choice about the food. First came fatback; next, white bread; then collard greens, peas, stewed tomatoes, one upon the other. Moultrie and Spoons sat down at a long, wooden table. Moultrie picked at the cornbread. Spoons nursed a glass of tea. Waiting.

Two men sat down directly across from them. One, tall and wide with a melon head. The other small, formed of sharp angles and horn-rimmed glasses.

"This is Beauchampes and Brown. They've known Shebrar a long time," Spoons said.

Moultrie gave a faint smile, nod. Beauchampes was looking down at his plate. Brown smiled back. He drank down one glass of milk. Six more stood by his plate, which was piled two inches deep in peanut butter. At its center lay a golden eye of syrup.

"What you got to say?" Beauchampes adjusted his glasses, looked at Spoons.

Moultrie knew he must take hold now. "They say you

88

aren't satisfied with the Muslim. They say you're wanting to—to cut around him."

"Who says that, brother?" Beauchampes said, looking out toward the Tunnel.

"There's a lot of talk here. If it's not so, you better stop it."

"You got awful big ears for a man that ain't been here long."

Brown laughed hard, his mouth full of peanut butter and syrup.

"Let's cut the crap," Moultrie snapped. "I'm here because I heard some of your pushers aren't happy. You're here because you think I can do something about it. I don't like the Muslim and you don't like the Muslim. So let's get it on."

Beauchampes sipped from his coffee. Prisoners opened the wide windows. The cold air was rushing into the cafeteria. The Yard bell sounded in the wind.

"Why, man, you ain't been here long enough not to like the Muslim. A man who dislikes a brother for no reason—he ain't no friend of mine."

Moultrie paused to eat a little cornbread. Thought coldly. "He's cutting the stuff. Taking some off the top and cutting the rest. Strychnine."

"That's a lie," Beauchampes said.

"Maybe so."

"Where'd you hear that?"

"People know."

Beauchampes took off his glasses and wiped them with a napkin. "I'd really like to know about your ears, man. I mean, I'd really like to find out about that."

"Throw in with me, you'll find out."

Beauchampes lit a cigarette, studying Moultrie's face. "Why should I help you?"

Moultrie's eyes flashed. "You're not helping me, I'm helping you. I got better contacts than he could ever have. He's been off the street too long. You help me get rid of the Muslim and we'll both make money. Whiskey's already behind me."

"Prove it."

"Check it."

"I'll do that. And you tell me why you're so set on getting rid of the Muslim. Is it—personal?"

"Purely business."

Brown had finished his breakfast. He licked his fingers.

"Right now, I could get an ounce off the street—uncut—five grand," Beauchampes said.

"Bullshit. But I *can* get you an uncut ounce for seven."

Beauchampes looked at his cigarette and flicked the ashes. "You name me a couple of street men."

"That's my business."

"Maybe you're trying to set me up."

"Could be," Moultrie said.

Beauchampes looked at him a moment, then slid his glasses into a leather case. Turned to Spoons. "What you say about a little poker some night, Spoons?"

"Sounds all right."

Beauchampes took his tray and left. Brown followed slowly.

Moultrie made sure they were out of sight before speaking. "What'd you think?"

"We wait and see. He's a smart cat."

Picking up their trays, they filed into the silver line. A wire cage collected the spoons and forks. The duty

90

guard was half asleep in cigarette smoke. In front of Moultrie a few old men palmed silverware into their jeans.

"What the hell's that all about?" Moultrie asked.

"Some new guys getting scared, jumpy. Don't know where to get weapons yet. So these old-timers sell them forks, spoons. Make knives out of them in the shops. I don't know—it's a bad sign. Maybe there *was* something to the beekeeper's dying."

"To hell with that! When will we know something about this deal?" Moultrie asked.

"Couple days. Meanwhile, you better stay out of the shadows."

12

MEALTIME. Beneath the blighted, buzzing lights of the cafeteria Walsh was pacing evenly up and down the long rows of wooden tables—"the pipeline," Cays called them. Under which at each meal jewelry, pictures, dope, even brass knuckles and knives were examined, passed along; bought and sold. "You watch the men, not the pipeline," Cays had told him and Walsh listened, realizing that he was in a sense training under Rhiner and Cays, who told him the usual schooling for new men was simple: "Stand in the Yard. Watch for fights."

Rhiner had made lieutenant in two years. Screw him. Walsh and Cays during this past week had headed cafeteria security, six men working beneath them. Still, now and then, Walsh felt his stomach flatten against his ribs as he patrolled fifteen hundred men fed in three shifts. When he corrected errors made against the rules that hung on long signs along the cafeteria's walls:

ABSOLUTELY NO SMOKING

and

ONE FORK, ONE SPOON

and

**SHIRT TAIL IN AND CAP OFF ARE
TWO KEYS TO THE WORLD**

and

**LIKE IT OR NOT, THIS IS YOUR HOME,
SO TREAT IT THAT WAY**

Lately he had begun a notebook, putting down those conditions about prison life he thought should be changed: better bathroom facilities; a game room for the prisoners; solid training for the guards. Some of his ideas he sent in letters to Patricia though his thoughts drifted—making love high in the frozen, rotting cupola above her mother's kitchen that smelled of simmering red beans and peppers, while the raw sea wind rattled the frozen panes about them, shattering the icicles, blowing in the sharp woodsmoke of Portland.

After cafeteria duty, Walsh and Cays often walked down the Tunnel and out to Shack One, the one-room building that held the middle of the Yard. The Yard, a large square covered in blacktop, was flanked on one side by the cafeteria and on the other by the infirmary. At the end of the Yard sat the huge red-brick Industry Building.

93

In Shack One they had long raps, now and again checking passes, always watching the movement of the men. Listening to Cays's rambling, twangy speeches, Walsh learned about the prison. Seventy percent of the prison was black. Most of the men were armed robbers and carried prison-made knives. "You ever feel a shiv on a man, you let him go. You don't try to take it off him or it's your guts on the floor. Give him a hard one-eye. Write a report. When we had clubs, it was different. We had a chance. But now—we just write a report." Armed robbers, at least with the white inmates, were the top social stratum and held murderers, rapists, common thieves below them. The blacks, according to Cays, who had worked in other prisons, usually had no structure. But here things were different. Here they were ruled by one man called the Muslim. "But that nigger's getting a hard time from this new buck—Moultrie. And it's bad. Bad for everybody here."

One afternoon, just after they had shaken down a few men in the yard, Walsh noticed a strange tension about Cays's face. "Feel a shiv on one of those guys?" he asked.

"More than that, bo," Cays answered quietly.

"What?"

"Nineteen fifty-seven. Same feeling. Three flapjacks fried in the chair. You ever seen a fry?"

The question threw Walsh off balance.

"You mean they never showed you movies of it in college?"

Walsh flushed and Cays caught him. "Aw, come on, buddy. You wear them books like a bowtie. We ain't that dumb."

Walsh said nothing.

94

Cays stuck his red thumbs into his green uniform pants, squinted his eyes, recalling. "Let's see. Back in fifty-seven—oh, I was 'bout your age, I guess. Twenty, twenty-one, and the slammer still had me pretty scared, so I didn't notice the building up, the bad growing, till I looked back on it. Chief Flanders, walking through the Yard, tried to break up a fight between a couple guys and they went woo-woo. Stabbed him thirty times or so with screwdrivers. Deader than Swiss cheese. Then the whole place went off. Army called in. Five or six prisoners shot. Couple more guards killed. After it was over, they had a trial in two weeks. Most of the prisoners got off with light sentences. Three got death. Two niggers, one white. I was with them the last night and morning."

Cays went on in his nasal though now hushed tones, and Walsh envisioned the story, felt it as if he were there.

It is 7 P.M. on the evening of their death. Three men are waiting in the death house. They have just come from the showers, each carefully watched while he bathed. Forced to use soap and wire sponges. You must be clean to die. You may shave tonight or wait until five in the morning. Death comes at six. Death will rise with the sun, out of the black river, death.

Supper arrives. Shallow broth and tea. No bread or meat. Nothing that can be discharged at six. Little is eaten. Four cells directly face the chair. The chair is painted white and is larger than they expected and encased in glass. They have never seen the chair before, except one on a school tour when he was a boy. Leather belts, steel buckles. The copper head plate gleaming beneath one light bulb. They search for other things. From the wall hangs the phone and life. Beside it, on a wooden

95

peg, lies a broad strip of leather used over sixty times—the death mask. There are two mirrors in the left- and right-hand corners of the chamber. A full-length two-way mirror is implanted in the wall. The executioner will be behind it early. Some wonder if he waits there now. Watching. Doing whatever it is they do in the night.

Time, time. One man cries. Another throws up what he can. Then dry heaves. One begins masturbating, but is stopped. Masturbation is not permitted before you die. Farther down from these cells there is a boiling and hissing. Later in the night a tearing and dry ripping as of cloth. A smell of salt cutting through the air. They wonder at these noises, the odor, but they will not be told the origin. Sleep is a word, or something in the shadows. Sleep is somewhere in the shadows waiting beneath the chair, but will not rise for them until the sun rises. The hours hold on as long as they can and then expire. The men listen for sounds but hear none other than the low hissing, and so remember those sounds most familiar to them—not of children's coughs, or wives turning in bed, or tumbling rains, or secret snows, but rather they remember the tiers at night: the sound of steam rustling through cranky pipes and leaking in steady rhythm upon the floor; the tiny voice of the night guards' radio blinking in the darkness; hard, sawing snores and heavy moanings against springs, rusty and complaining; the sound of one fallen into some cold pit of sleep, fighting his way back to a lesser darkness; one pacing quickly and one pacing slowly; fingers snapping against the bars like dry paper fans; the easy turning of a book; the clicking on and off of lights; the bony rattle of dice against the stone; the wicked shuttling and carving of a penknife, and these shavings falling even, like a brown and sapling snow. These things they remember.

It is five o'clock now and their hearts beat differently than ever before. A guard opens each cell, locks it behind the prison barber who shaves heads and faces with the clattering electric razor, asking each man: "How much hair on your belly and butt?" If there is much, the prisoner is shaved clean.

Five thirty and the white suits are brought in. The men slide into the stiff cotton, shiver with the cold. The taste for smoke and coffee arises. One cigarette per man. No coffee. But the cigarette is enough. It is life and fills their lungs sweetly.

Quarter to six, and they are led by a guard one by one to the latrine.

"Go."

"I can't."

"Try. It'll be easier for you."

"Give me a couple seconds."

The seconds flash.

"Anything?"

"A little. Will it be enough?"

"Oh, God. I guess."

Back to the cell. More lights flicking on. The chaplain asks if they want prayer. Two yes, one no. Always the Twenty-third Psalm.

Five minutes until six and the first cell door quietly opens. He feels the guard's arms gently about him. Still he hears the hissing somewhere. Cold concrete against his bare feet. The white suit too tight. From his crotch rushes a sudden stream of urine. Blinks apologetically toward the guard, not feeling it coming. Down into the chair. Straps cinched over his wrists, chest, belly, legs. Breathing high in his chest, he looks at one guard.

"Will it hurt?"

The guard pales, averts his eyes.

"Oh, Jesus. Is it going to burn me?"

"Naw . . . naw, it's . . . alright now."

But he does feel the sharp electrode pricking into his left ankle, his wrist. In the plate glass he sees himself, without hair, thin, in the big chair. The copper plate fastens to his head. Cold. His pants are wet and he has no hair. Feels ashamed of his bony and yellow naked feet. He didn't mean to wet his pants. Then the leather mask comes down. Darkness. It covers up to his forehead and beneath his chin. His nose fits into a notch but there are no holes for breathing. He must suck in the air from below his chin. Sounds like a whistle. He is whistling in the chair. Then suddenly on top of his skull, across his feet and ankles rushes a warmth. The current he thinks, and it is over. But only the salt water which has been boiling in the iron pot all night. His feet are lifted. Rags torn the night before are dipped into the bucket of salt water, packed under them.

Two minutes till six and the Warden arrives. The witness box has filled. A doctor waits with his stethoscope. The sun is rising. He can hear coughs from those watching him. Rustling. The ticking of the Warden's watch. Popping of leather straps as he trembles. Cold saliva dripping down his chin while he still sucks, whistles for air.

Thirty seconds. With his back to the chair the Warden glances up toward the left mirror. Prisoner is quiet. Toward the right. Witnesses assembled. Six o'clock. With

98

one swift motion of his right hand he signals the executioner. His own image reflected back to him from the mirror, and the volts hit.

"Ma!!" screams the blank leather mask. There are two more jolts. No more screams. Two more men.

Walsh still smelled the salt water, seemed to hear the ticking of the watch, when Cays's face blurred back into view—cold, his eyes dull and slow.

"I read this book one time about dogs. Fancy dogs. They use a needle on them when they get sick, or too old. Just stick them and it's over in twenty seconds," Cays said.

"An executioner," Walsh murmured. "I just don't see how a man could . . ."

"Ole Hap Davis. I knew him good and he was a fine man. A Christian man. Said he never smoked a live one. Said every one of them was dead before he hit the chair."

"This was in fifty-seven?" Walsh asked.

"About then. But there's a feeling I got now, like when this place blew before. Like I'm about to choke or something. Like everybody's about to choke."

They looked out toward the Tunnel and the cold walls of the Yard and the guntowers whistling in the wind.

13

F o r three or four days it had been raining, but today the Yard was brimming full of sunlight. Childs could smell many things . . . leaves, stone, the blowing earth. He and the rest of the crew approached two large trucks idling by the barrels of garbage. Apple cores lay on top of the cans and at first Childs was afraid. But in a few minutes, he was rolling barrels down the loading ramp, throwing his higher and faster than anyone else. The bees circled above his head. The smell of the slop cans made him feel good today. Just as he threw a barrel up, a big black man, captain of the crew, asked him:

"Where your gloves, boy?"

"I don't have none."

"You work this job, you got to wear gloves."

Childs felt bad. Felt that he had let the captain down.

"Do I have to go in?"

The captain looked around, then pulled Childs behind a pile of barrels. "You got a roommate?"

"No."

"I'm coming by some night after Count. You tell the tier boy to leave your cell open, peach ass. What's the number?"

"Twenty-seven."

The captain put a hand through his blond hair and tugged. "Don't you forget."

"Don't you pull my hair."

"For now, peach ass. Just for now." He put on his big, bad-smelling gloves and went back on the truck.

Childs thought to himself that he did not like this man. He reminded him of those men on the third tier. Once he almost told John Hawkins about what had happened on the third tier, but he was afraid that he would laugh at him like the guards did.

They worked about an hour loading slop cans on the trucks. Sometimes the younger men would pull apart and pretend they were fighting. As they boxed, they made noises, just below whistles, wide smiles spreading on their faces, never really touching one another. Then abruptly they would break apart and turn to trade licks with the wind.

After the garbage trucks were filled, the men hung their gloves on a rack by the cafeteria and went back to their cells. Childs hid behind some barrels until he saw the captain go in. Then, feeling the heat of the sun, the energy, he spun around. It felt good. The sun made a nest of clean light around him and he spun around again. Then he heard something: a familiar sound from behind the empty barrels where he had hidden from the captain. He turned toward the pile and heard it again louder, his heart thumping like quail. He knew the sound well, and his first impulse was to rush toward the short, high yips. Then he thought more clearly and moved quietly toward the fence behind the garbage bin. There, in a tall patch of weeds, he saw the puppy. It sat thin and dark, with enormous eyes that ran in the sun. It would howl and then shiver, cocking its ears for any sound. Childs knew how to handle it. He lay down on his belly and eased toward the fence.

In tower seven, a guard, watching Childs, took his gun down from the rack.

He spoke gently to the puppy. Stretched a hand through the fence. His sleeve caught. He brought his arm back and rolled up the sleeve.

The guard, unnoticed, flipped his dark glasses down and eased out on the gunboards.

Childs put his bare arm through the fence. "Come on, puppy; come on, boy. I ain't going to hurt you." The puppy moved farther into the weeds. Childs got up from the ground. Food, he thought. A little bread would bring him here. He walked into the dark trash bin.

The guard, keeping his shotgun low, looked where Childs had been stretching his hand.

Inside the bin, steam hissed and rushed from a stained conduit. Childs let his eyes adjust to the dark. He was impatient with his eyes because they took so long to see. *He will be gone. His mother will come for him.* As his eyes searched the trash pile, he saw a movement at the far end of the building. Two men stood knee-deep in garbage in front of the steam pipe. At first, he thought

102

they were looking at him, but they were not. They spoke to one another. He could not hear what they said because they spoke softly. Childs's vision grew better. One of them was a tall, round guard. As far as Childs could tell the other was a boy. The guard did a strange thing: he pulled his pants down and turned his face into the steam and then he turned back around and cocked his hat on the boy's head. The boy smoothed his hands across the guard's butt, moved in behind him and for a moment, they said small, quiet things.

When Childs saw that they were not watching, he moved quickly outside but stopped suddenly when he saw a rind of meat near the bin. He picked it up and went back to the fence. Lay down flat on his belly and dangled the meat in front of the puppy. In a second he had him through the fence and in his arms.

The guard grinned to himself, went back into the tower, and put his gun away.

Childs hid the puppy in his shirt. It licked at his belly and made him laugh. As he walked through the Yard, he felt very happy. His blue work shirt bulged only slightly with the puppy. It did not move. *It is asleep. It is my heart that makes it sleep.*

A young black man was pulling a red wagon across the Yard. He waved at Childs, who waved back. He came close to Childs with the wagon. It was filled with oranges and candy bars. Childs could smell them.

"Hey, how about an orange?" the other asked.

Childs was afraid he would see the puppy. He sucked his stomach in. "No." From somewhere behind him he could smell a strange odor. When he turned, a very thin man dodged in between him and the vendor. He picked out two small oranges.

"How much?" he asked.

"Nothing for you," the vendor muttered. As the tall man was limping away, the vendor made a sign on himself, like a cross.

Childs thought he saw the vendor shudder. He looked away for a moment and then back at Childs, wiping his hands across his jeans.

"You ought to try one. You ain't had one like this," he said.

Childs backed toward the Tunnel door. "I got to go," he said, barely breathing, keeping a hand over his stomach.

"You don't look too good. Something the matter with your belly?"

In his cell, Childs made a bed for the puppy out of a shoebox lined with rags. He fed it mashed oatmeal cookies and water, and the puppy slept. Childs lay down, too. Just before he went to sleep, he thought of the strange boy and the guard in the steam. Remembered Buckie Belser: taking off one another's clothes and hugging, high on the swarthy cotton bales, jammed in close against the tin roof, so high in the loud, sweaty, working darkness of the mill. . . .

A tapping at the bars woke him up.

"Well, at least you get to lay around between trucks," John Hawkins said. "Here. I brought your paint." He set the cans by the bunk.

Childs showed Hawkins the puppy. But the Hawk said he should get rid of it. That most men in here didn't like dogs. *I'll do what I want.*

104

Childs was dragging the broad brush across the stone. Liked the feeling, the smell of painting.

"This weather—it really gets to me. It's fishing weather, you know. You fish?"

"My daddy and me. The mill pond had bass," Childs said.

"Fall's the best time, alright. The water's low and clear."

A little breeze, crisp as apples, stirred through the broken window. For a time they talked of the big fall picnics the mill owners threw. About barbecue and cider and the local heroes of arm wrestling and spool rolling.

"Hey, they got a movie tonight in the cafeteria. You want to go?" John Hawkins asked.

"I got to do some sewing. Besides, this fella might come by and I'm going to tell him off."

"Who?"

"He's real big and works on the trucks. He pulled my hair today."

Staring at Childs, John Hawkins sealed the paint can. "Is he the big black guy? Is he captain of the crew?"

"Yeah."

"God Almighty, Childs! Do you know who that is? Do you know what he's coming for?"

"I don't like him. He smells bad."

"He's coming here to screw you, Childs! That nigger's J. L. Stuckey, and he's coming to ream your ass!"

Childs lowered his eyes. He did not understand why John Hawkins said such things.

Hawkins flopped down on the bunk. "Jesus Christ! Is there something the matter with you?"

Childs checked on the puppy. He still slept. He sat

105

down beside Hawkins and folded his hands. "I will lock my door."

"Shit. He'll get to the tier boy. That ain't the way to keep him out. What time is he coming?"

"Just some night, he said."

Hawkins put his face in his hands and looked at his shoes. "There's something we can do. Just don't run scared. I know some guys. They don't know you yet. They don't feel responsible yet, but Stuckey's a nigger. That helps. That helps a lot. Listen—what I got to do is talk to these guys."

"Who?"

"Just these guys I know. Now you got to keep your mouth shut about it. There's ways to stop this kind of thing, but we need help."

"I can do it myself. I'm not so slow."

"You go ahead and do what you want. Just keep your mouth shut and don't go to the screws. Got that? I can get you out of this—unless . . ." Hawkins was searching Childs's eyes. "Unless you don't want out of it."

Childs's face was clean.

"Well, I'll see you this afternoon. You don't worry. I'll get us some help, somehow," he said, easing out the door.

Maybe I should try to find Stuckey. Maybe I should let him have it. I'm not so slow.

But he knew these were bad thoughts and so he opened his arms, began saying the strange words that came to him as a boy. The lights winked and glowed in him. Once, when he was younger, he dreamed the lights asked him what he wanted more than anything else in the world. To be a good tradesman, he said. To be a boot-

106

maker. And then he told his deepest secret to them. He wanted to be good enough to make beautiful black slippers for the young princes he had seen in a picture book. In the dream, the lights promised his wish. You're not so slow, they seemed to say.

14

NEARING six o'clock in the evening, suppertime, and before the warden goes home, he decides to shave, while they are creeping by his door, quiet as cats—murderers— slipping just outside the bathroom. Baring his neck for the safety razor, tilting his head back and to the left, he just catches a glimpse of the blades and black hands snatching his head backward, the wide, full neck opening like a bloom, red, from ear to ear, and hot blood gushes like a bucket over his white shirt, steaming into the basin. . . .

Walsh had read the morning newspaper account of the downstate warden's murder only once, but the story kept circling his head, and he wondered how the prisoners here took it—two black men killed, the other two captured. As for the guards—the Count bells had rung breakfast some time ago but the cell blocks had not been opened. Second shift had been placed on alert and there was talk of keeping the prisoners off the playing field even though it was Sunday. Chief Freeman had called a meeting.

"It's gone too far for anything else. They ought to take those two niggers and burn them like black cats. What bothers me is that they got him in his office. Now, how did that happen?" Creekland's face was tight, nervous.

Rhiner, shaking his head: "It's a bad thing. Everybody will pay for this one."

Creekland turned to Walsh. "What do you think?"

"They should get tough out there," Walsh said.

"Get tough, hell. They should throw them in the chair. And I'll tell you one thing—Jesse Cates, he better make damn sure his door's locked or maybe I'll take a crack at him. Damned if I'm going out on that playing field today. Not with them prisoners thinking they can get away with anything. They've heard the news. What do you bet they been drinking and screwing and laughing about it all morning?"

Behind them guards filed up the stairs to the meeting.

"Well, let's go on up there and see what the warden thinks about all this," Rhiner said.

"Hell, I know what he thinks—'Git on out to the field, boys. The prisoners need their exercise, boys!' Damned if I will!"

Walsh followed them to the Countroom where Chief Freeman was waiting, hands crossed behind his back. He chewed on his cigar while the remaining men sat down. Then he spoke smoothly and clear.

109

"We've all heard the news and so have the cons. The ward keepers say things are tight down there, but not too bad. I've talked to Warden Cates. He thinks if we keep them locked up, it'll be worse. I'll listen to opinions."

Creekland's keys rattled in his chair. Everyone looked at him as he stood up. "As long as we got them in the cell blocks, we can watch them. Something goes wrong there and we can do something about it. Outside, we got six towers. If those men get spooked, chances are they'll cut right through them fences, taking four or five of us with them. I say it's crazy to go out there."

Freeman relit his cigar. "Anybody else? Alright, we got sixteen second-shift men coming in. We're putting them in the killing zone with Brownings. That should discourage any break. Anybody else worried?"

Creekland mumbled something.

"They'll have live ammo, right?" someone called out.

"Yep," Freeman said, looking at the men carefully. "Rhiner here will have ten men with him on the field today. I'll assign the rest when you get out there. That's all, gentlemen."

The playing field was wide and green. Its sprinklers had just been cut off and the grass sparkled. Already the second-shift guards paced in the killing zone, carrying Browning shotguns that caught the light. Rhiner spread his men widely over the field. Told them not to bunch up. Told Walsh if there was trouble, shooting, to lie down flat. But Walsh was not interested in listening to Rhiner. He had thought out Peterson's situation. The guy seemed straightforward, genuinely afraid. So he had decided to ask Rhiner about Peterson again, this time wanting more than a clipped no. He turned his attention to the field.

110

Most of the men had filtered out. Some of them went to the shack and took out bats and balls. They set out the bases and began a game. Others played handball or horseshoes or touch football. Now and then, they all had their eyes on the guards.

Walsh eased over to the horseshoe pit. Ten or twelve men stood around this long, red wound in the grass. The man who was throwing had only one hand and hung the extra horseshoes on his stump, so that it turned red, like the clay. When he threw, he whistled like a bomb and exploded on ringers. Some of the men clapped at the ringers, but most stared at Walsh.

A big stove rested in the left corner of the field. The cooks had built a good fire in it and were fixing apple turnovers. Walsh could tell the cooks were nervous; they kept wiping their hands at their aprons and scratching at their heads. Rhiner was slouching by the stove, eating an apple turnover, when Walsh walked over to him.

"Any good?"

"It's alright. Could use a little more sugar."

"Give me one," Walsh said to a cook.

The cook filled a piece of dough with cooked apples and sugar. Walsh would have told him not to put the sugar in, but it was too late.

"Damn white sugar will kill you," he said, pacing himself, not wanting to speak too quickly. He and Rhiner viewed the playing field. Most of the men sat and talked among themselves. The air smelled of the river and the cooked apples.

"Looks pretty quiet," Walsh said.

"Never can tell. Maybe so, though."

The cook handed Walsh his turnover. He took a bite, burnt his lips. He let it cool. Waiting.

Rhiner finished, wiped his mouth. "Okay, what's the gripe?"

"You're wrong on Peterson. He should be moved."

"Thought about it, huh?"

"A little."

"Let me tell you something. You're doing alright here. Moving up faster than you think and that makes me look good, too, see? Oh, you're still a little straight maybe, but you'll learn about that. About the way things work— the way they got to work. One thing, though—nobody likes molesters. Not cons, not screws, not the Warden. You get your hands dirty with Peterson, and you kiss a couple quick promotions bye-bye."

"Got me pegged, huh?"

"I know the animal. When he's hungry, he moves like he's hungry."

"I just might surprise you, Rhiner."

"Maybe," Rhiner said. He pulled his hat down to the bridge of his nose, moving back out into the field. "Maybe."

By late afternoon, all seemed well. Many of the men were playing ball or running laps. At four o'clock, Rhiner stood in the center of the field and blew a whistle. The men began to put away equipment and headed for the buildings.

At the entrance to Building Two, there was a sudden commotion. Walsh could hear someone screaming "Fight!" Fifty or sixty men surged into the building. The prisoners on the field began dropping equipment and running toward Building Two, which lay behind the

112

double fences. In the killing zone, the second shift fell back and raised their guns. The guards on the field pulled into a tight group. Rhiner signaled them to break up, but they did not.

Chief Freeman stood on an outside catwalk holding a phone to his ear. Rhiner ran toward him. Walsh followed.

"Big?" Rhiner asked out of breath.

"Fight in Building Two," Freeman said. "They got Thomas. Dumb bastard tried to break it up. Looks like they want to keep him for a while."

"Give me ten men. I'll get him out," Rhiner said.

"I don't want to scare them into making this something it's not. I need you out there on the field."

"I can do it," Walsh said. His knees felt weak.

"He's a good man. He can do the job," Rhiner said, looking at Walsh.

"No."

"Look, he's new. They can't figure him. He could bluff."

Freeman paused, tugged at his cigar, and flicked ashes on the ground. He turned to Rhiner. "Give second shift orders to cut down any man that moves for the fences and get your men the hell off that field."

Rhiner nodded. He winked at Walsh, then ran down the catwalk.

Freeman picked up the phone. "I want two men and three shotguns. I want them in the Gateroom quick." He hung up and looked at Walsh. "Alright, come on!"

Walsh follows him to the Gateroom. Two guards are waiting with the shotguns. Freeman gives Walsh one of the guns.

"You don't give them time to think. Tell them you

want Thomas now, and there won't be any deals. Got it?"

"Yes, sir," Walsh says. Things he wants to ask. No time. Moving quickly toward Building Two. Radiators whistle along the walls. Sun jumping across the tall windows, and for the first time Walsh notices potted plants on the sills.

Freeman motions the other two guards ahead. At the entrance to the Tunnel, pulls something out of his pocket and gives it to Walsh. A shotgun shell.

"Most of these guys know we don't carry loaded weapons in there. This is your ace. You bluff with it. If you have to, blow the ceiling down. But—and get this straight—you don't shoot anybody. You don't blow anybody away. You just bluff." He studies Walsh's eyes a moment, then goes to the third section gate.

Walsh holding the shotgun. Shoving in the shell. Stomach churning, feeling a little sick. He has to go through with it now.

Freeman waits at the gate. Around him six guards with clubs, mace.

"You do what Walsh says. You watch his back," Freeman says to the other two guards, opening the gate. Then to Walsh, "Remember—I can be there fast. Two minutes and I can have twenty men with Thompsons in there."

Walsh, through the gate, hearing it clang behind him, the steps of the men following, hears loose change in their pockets, smells nothing but the Browning's blued barrel and holds it closer, tighter, walking ahead. Building Two, but the door is locked. One of the other guards opens it with a steel key.

Be cool, play this thing right. "You guys can just stand here. I think I got it."

114

"Freeman said to watch your back."

"You just stay here. You don't let them lock the door on me." Thinking now, cocks the hat on the back of his head, carries the Browning in his right hand. Feels his left hand shaking, so sticks it into his pocket, moving in. The ward in disarray: paint smeared on the walls; broken windows; water flooding the floor, wetting his feet. Toward the back, seventy-five or eighty men waiting behind the barricade of bunks. As he moves toward them, they begin to shout names, throw books, shoes, and now he is in it as much as they. Something stings his right hand, but he keeps going straight for them, shotgun slung against his side. A few feet away, he stops, scanning them all, feeling himself squaring his hat. "Thomas? You here?"

Silence. Takes out his left hand and puts it on his hip. "Thomas?"

"I'm here! Behind the bunks in here!"

"You alright?"

"Yeah."

A thin white man steps out from the bunks. "You want something, screw?"

"Thomas."

F. W. Rosline looks back over his shoulder, smiles. "Well, I don't think you're going to get him right now, screw."

"I do," Walsh says softly.

"With an empty gun? Far as I can remember, state law says you can't bring a loaded weapon in here, 'less you got the Governor's say so. I don't think you got that."

"Give me Thomas or I'll cut you in half."

"With what? You got a pair of scissors on you?"

The rest of the prisoners are laughing, moving closer, holding pieces of pipe and wood, showing their knives.

"There's something that's got to be said. See, there was a fight going on in here. A good one. Two guys were getting something out of their systems . . ."

"You got five seconds." Walsh clicks off the safety.

". . . and this screw, see, he pokes his big nose in where he shouldn't . . ."

Walsh brings the gun to his hips and fires. Plaster sprays the room. Two lights pop out. Rosline stumbles back. Walsh moves up quickly, levels the shotgun just out of Rosline's reach, sighting in right between the eyes.

"Thomas," he says again, softly.

Watching the cold barrel aimed at his head, Rosline motions with his arm and Thomas jumps out from the barricade.

Walsh kept his bead on Rosline and eased back toward the door. "You guys shouldn't make such a mess. Clean it up!" He turned his back, laid the shotgun across his shoulder.

"Jesus Christ!" Thomas said. "You could have got us both killed!"

"Could have," Walsh said.

A crowd of guards gathered at the section gate.

"What happened in there?" Freeman asked.

Walsh held the shotgun out to him. "You got some holes in your ceiling."

Freeman stuck his cigar in his mouth and looked at the shotgun. "Basic rule, Mr. Walsh—when you fire a weapon, you clean it."

"Yes, sir," Walsh said. Tucking the shotgun under his arm, heading toward the Arsenal, he could feel the other

116

guards watching him. From the crowd, someone shouted: "Give 'em hell, Walsh!" And he felt a newness, an addition. A worth that he had not sensed here before, a belonging and pride.

15

To m Parker welded another seam into the car and finally got around to the point.

"See, I been married a good while, Father. And you know here, you don't get to do nothing but hug your wife once in a while. Just peck her on the cheek in the visiting room. So, I guess I kind of picked up some bad habits."

"You screwing somebody, Parker?" Breen asked, sticking out his big chin.

Parker crimsoned. "No. Nothing like . . ."

"You getting screwed by somebody?"

"Good God, no, Father. It's nothing like that. I wouldn't even think of that."

"Good. Give me that torch." Breen turned the flame up broad and yellow and singed a rusted spot. It turned smooth and clean. "Something about heat. Smooths it right out. You probably knew about that."

"Yeah, thanks. Looks nice. But the thing is I'm not doing none of those things you said, but a lot of something else. Seeing that I'm married and all, you think it's alright?"

"Nope. I don't," Breen clipped.

"But, Father—it's hard here."

"You think just because you're locked up, anything goes?"

"No."

"When's the last time you went to confession?"

"Couple months."

"Too long. I'll hear it now." Breen waved a cross. Parker automatically blessed himself. "Right here?"

"Right here."

"With everybody looking?"

"They won't hear a word."

Two men working on the front of the state patrol car ground out the demolished grill.

Breen gave Parker absolution. Put on a welding mask and spot welded a section of the crushed bumper to the car. The brace that had held up the bumper crashed to the floor. "Saves a little space," he said.

In the cold wind of the Yard, Breen was wiping some grease from his hands on a handkerchief. Some of the men were let out from the shops early. They huddled against the warm flanks of the buildings, stamping their feet. Hitching their shoulders. Rolling their hands into their pockets because of the cold. The scent of cooking rice and beans sifted out of the bright kitchens.

In the marshland, by the river's other side, night

119

gathered like a different flood. First-shift guards were drifting into the Yard with their brown lunch bags empty as their stomachs. Puffing their cigarettes and ready to go home.

How many times had he seen this image before in a deep sleep at night, or in a cold swirling of thought. Seen it from these buildings which for so long had gathered night into themselves. Night pouring into the red clay that imprisons these men now. The same clay even now rolling down the Broad River. Clay with which as children they fashioned mudpies in the embrace of soft summer. And on which at eighteen when their veins stung wild blood they laid their first long-legged woman. And into which, far in the lessening light, when all things have come to frost and fading, their bodies will be laid down to red dust, past all regions which they could have known or guessed at. To lie at last in a fine, mineral fastness, which packs along deep ravines or flows through the Broad River, or stands and gathers night in the form of these cold buildings. This prison dark where men leave forever some portion of themselves. Some frail image bound fast against stone and iron. While in their spirits rise countless rooms and locks, dark and cold, where they lie lost, like hide-and-seek children in the pathless woods, weeping.

The chapel bells tolling six o'clock brought Breen back. Watching the men and the guards stirring closely together, Breen felt a loneliness, a sleeping thirst welling up from his bones, but he pushed it back: *as if he could do something for them. As if anyone could.* He shivered, decided to get a workout in the gym.

*   *   *

"Damn," White said, picking himself up from the floor of the ring.

"You al—al—alright?"

"Where'd you pull that one from, Eddie? Never saw it coming."

"Le—le—le—," the black man slobbered, wiped his mouth, took a deep steadying breath. "Le—left. Co—coming at you low." He crouched, in slow motion repeating the action.

"It's a good shot. Come on. Put them up," White said, his feet cutting sharp angles across the mat.

Eddie Baldrick lunged in a quick left–right. White ducked away, landed a sound left, but took a jab in the face that stunned him. Then felt a hand snatch him back toward the ropes.

"Baldrick, get your ass out of this ring!" Breen said, leveling a finger at the prisoner's face.

Immediately, Baldrick began tugging off his gloves.

"Wait a minute, Eddie. Hold on." White grabbed Breen by the arm, turned him around. "You just don't come in here and order people around like that, Breen."

Breen's face flushed. He turned to Baldrick again. "I said beat it! You know the rules around here."

Eddie Baldrick jumped out of the ring.

"Yeah, well, maybe you'd like to fill me in," White said, his face tense, defiant.

"No physical contact between employees and prisoners," said Breen, hitching up his pants, gritting his teeth.

"He *needs* somebody to talk to."

"Confession begins at seven thirty A.M."

"This ring's his confessional!" White slammed a glove

onto the mat. "This ring's the only place he can talk. All he knows. The words get jammed up any place else, especially when guards run around blasting down dormitories."

"You're under obedience, White. Now shut your mouth and get out of here."

"Maybe you'd like to try and put me out."

Breen spread his feet, dug both hands into his hips, and looked at the floor. "I'm telling you to get out, buddy," he said.

The veins were throbbing at White's neck. He pushed Breen backward. "You should be a cop in South Boston like you were born to be. You want me out, put me out!"

Shoving his hands into Baldrick's gloves, Breen could feel the still-warm sweat. He had stripped off his shirt and shoes. "Ready?"

White nodded and moved in for him, loosing a shot from his right.

Breen ducked clear away, smiling.

White danced back in, throwing a hand to the gut, but missing the head shot.

Unhurt, Breen tried the one–two, but both were blocked, and this time White was smiling, tapping out of range.

Maneuvering White into the corner, Breen leaned to the right, then smoked a hard left.

White went down, but quickly came up again. A little blood trickled from his left eye.

Breen was feeling exhilarated. *Fifty, by God, and I can still salt them down. Maybe I should have been a cop.*

White was bobbing, weaving grimly to the right, planning a hook, when Breen's reach caught him again in the gut, then to the side of the head. Down to his knees, the room spinning.

Not until he saw the blood oozing from White's eye and nose did Breen ask himself what the hell he was doing. "Maybe . . . maybe we should call it even."

White was wobbling up, wiping his nose. Smearing his face and glove in blood. "What's the matter? Too tough for you?"

Breen pounded his gloves together. Came straight into White, but took a round between the eyes, felt his knees give.

As White was trying to follow up, he felt the first punch, but not the second. He was down.

"Good God!" someone said from the entrance to the gym. Two prisoners and a guard stared at the priests in the ring. One of them on his knees, the other still standing with his hands up. Both out of breath, smeared with blood.

Breen looked at himself and then at White. Slowly, he pulled off his gloves. "There's some guys . . . ah . . . White, there's some guys who want to box."

White wiped his nose. Dragged his gloves across the mat. Still on his knees, he turned to look at the guard and inmates. Painfully, he pushed himself up. "Yeah," he said, squinting through the blood. "Yeah. It's . . . all yours." With his gloves still on, he staggered out of the ring, stumbled out the side door to the rectory.

Breen climbed down. He looked at the men, glanced back at the ring, stuck his hands into his pockets. He shrugged and tried to smile. "You need gloves—anything like that?"

"No, Father," the guard said.

Breen wiped at an eyebrow, rubbing the sweat into his pants. "Just cut off the lights when you leave. Saves the Warden a little dough." He turned to go.

"Father?" one of the prisoners said.

"Yeah?"

"Was that for real?"

Breen looked over his shoulder toward the ring.

16

CHILDS had not worked for two days. The Hawk said that it was not safe for him. He told Childs that he was doing all he could, not to worry. So when the building sergeant came up to his cell, Childs said that he was sick, wasn't able to work. "Just losing money," the sergeant said, and Childs felt ashamed. The knife John Hawkins had left for him felt smooth and cool in his hand, though he decided not to take it to the cafeteria. Besides, he did not want to cut Stuckey or anyone else.

Today the Tunnel had a clean wind moving through it, and high outside the windows of its ceiling mocking birds were singing. But for the first time since he had come here, he saw that the Tunnel's section gates had been closed off. A guard waited at each gate. Childs was carefully shaken down three times and the guards did not smile or talk to him. They were changing. Since Sunday, since the fight and that shotgun blast, something had gotten up under their eyes and faces and was crawling around, like rats in feed bags. It made him uneasy.

Oh, I've dreamed about him. You better believe I have, but I never really thought he'd be mine. Never thought I'd get his sweet ass into my cell. There's something about him, though. I just can't decide, least not yet, whether he's really smart, I mean can figure you out like a slide rule, or whether he's dumb—well, innocent, whatever you want to call it. And that's unusual for me, 'cause I've seen them all, honey. And the ones I ain't seen, I have heard about. Sometimes when I'd pick up my sewing (oh, hell, I can sew. I just tore up some old clothes so I could see his sweet ass) I'd ask him some silly know-nothing question, and then he'd get that soft, dreamy look in his eyes, saying he didn't understand— what you mean, baby, I could eat it up with a spoon! Makes me shiver to think about it. Maybe that's why I want him so much—those sweet blue eyes, that kind of 'help me, I'm confused' innocence. Not that his body doesn't pull me like a pair of pliers! Oh, darling, the thought of those railroad shoulders and that wicked waist has kept me up all night sometimes. And it's a sound business move, too. The boys in this prison would pay a hundred bucks a trick for that straw-waisted buck. Well, for all I know he was captain of his high-school football team and made it with every cheerleader in the state. We'll see. You just give ole Montana a little bit of time, she'll find out whether he's faking it or not. To tell

126

you the truth, I hope he's dumb as the driven snow. Some of the girls like football players or army boys or preachers. But you just give me a dumb, tall, broad, tow-headed sapling, just apumping and arunning all that unused farmboy sap through those biceps and those beautiful, carved, brown-haired legs and that randy, hot farm-boy back—sugar, you give me that, and I'll give you this part of my soul for that piece of paradise!

Childs smuggled some sausage scraps and cornbread back from the cafeteria. The puppy ate them quickly. In the past long week it had grown larger and needed a name. Weeds, he decided on, because it ate so much and he had found it in the weeds. Lately Childs had become aware of time. Of how different it was here. How slow and cold it seemed to be. He still had almost the whole five years to do and felt sad. He set the puppy up on his bed. Weeds helped to take away the sad thoughts. For a while they played tug of war with an old sock. Then Weeds got too mean and Childs bit him on the nose like his daddy had said to do. The puppy pissed on the bed and curled up and went to sleep. Childs wiped up the dampness and worked on his sewing. Thinking about the big Catholic minister he had seen stomping through the Tunnel, wearing a muddy sweat suit and tennis shoes. A few men waiting in the lunch line looked harshly toward the man they called Breen and said that he had better wise up and not be so tough on White. That he wasn't as big as he thought. Some other men ahead in line had turned around then and told them to watch their mouths.

"Danny?"

"Yes."

"It's me, Montana. I'm a little early."

"Come on in," Childs said. Montana Red had given him some extra sewing. He felt sorry for Montana because all his clothes were so old, so he did not charge him much.

Montana Red stepped into the cell. Smelled sweet, and the rhinestone was glittering in his ear.

"It's not quite finished yet."

"Just give me what you have."

Childs gave him one shirt. Montana saw the puppy and asked where he got him. Childs told the story. Montana said that maybe he ought to get rid of him, though. Childs asked why, and Montana said that there was a guy named John Darcy who lived in this building and didn't like dogs. Childs did not answer. They talked about the room for a while. Montana said that he had some nice curtains that would go with the blue just right. He talked about fixing up the cell until Childs interrupted.

"I got a problem. You told me to ask if I had a problem."

"Okay. Let's hear it."

Childs summoned his courage. "There's a man named Stuckey. John Hawkins says he's going to screw me."

"Do you want him to?"

"He smells bad. Once, he pulled my hair."

Montana asked if Childs had tried to talk to Stuckey. Childs said that he had not. Montana said that it might help and that you ought to do that.

"It wasn't a game when he pulled my hair. He meant it to hurt."

"If you have some money, that will do. I know this guy. He'll leave you alone for money."

"How much?"

"Couple hundred, probably."

Childs shook his head.

"How about your parents?"

"Daddy worked in the carding room but he don't make enough."

Montana Red thought for a time. "I can do this for you. I can pay off this guy—but you have to pay me back."

Childs's face brightened. "I will."

Montana sat down beside him. "You have to do what I say. It won't be bad. I wouldn't ever hurt you."

"I know you wouldn't." Childs finished up a stitch. "I can work at night more. There's a lot of folks here that need mending done. I've seen their shirts."

"You won't have to do that, Danny. You just stay with me. We'll be friends, okay?"

"My room just got painted."

"You can repaint ours if you want."

"Can I bring my puppy?"

"Yes."

"The building sergeant won't let us change."

"Oh, I just have to do some sweet things for him, honey."

Down below the whistle blew for the trucks to be emptied. Childs got up to leave.

Montana Red caught him by the hand. "You don't worry about that anymore. You don't worry about anything now."

Childs put his sewing aside. The whistle blew and blew.

17

"'IT's crazy. It's a setup."

"Get your ass out of that bed and come on!"

Spoons got up, buckled the brace around his badly swollen leg. "We'll need knives then, goddammit."

"Can you get them through shakedown?" Moultrie asked.

"It's the Book Bindery, right? Creekland slaps your legs is all, there."

They laid the cold knives flat against their bellies. The blades were long, thin as marsh grass, made for close-in work, for stabbing.

As they moved through the Yard, Spoons's brace was scraping loudly.

"I heard you took a wrench and bummed your leg up bad, so you could stay locked up all day."

"I fell down," Spoons said. "That's all."

"Funny what you hear around this place. You got the passes?"

Spoons hated the way Moultrie picked at him. "I got them. But I can't figure why Beauchampes wants to meet in the Book Bindery."

"I bet it was whiskey getting behind us that made Beauchampes come across."

Spoons stopped just in front of the shakedown zone. "Listen, man, you better think about this. It's crazy. We shouldn't meet these guys here. It stinks."

"It's too late. We're this far. We go all the way," Moultrie said.

Spoons cursed under his breath.

They moved inside a large yellow circle painted on the pavement—the shakedown spot. The gate behind it led to the prison Industry Building. A young guard strolled out of the nearby shack. Moultrie sensed something about him.

"Watch it," Spoons whispered. "It ain't Creekland."

"Pass," the guard said.

They flashed the cards. The guard took them, then gave them back.

"What's your business here?"

"Inventory," Moultrie quickly said, sucking his belly and the knife flat.

"Inventory of what?"

"Binders."

"Okay, arms up."

They raised their hands and he slapped their sides and legs. They turned to leave.

"Hold it. What's that?" The guard pointed at Spoons's belly.

"What?" Spoons said.

"Those trousers aren't prison issue. Better get rid of them. Could get you into trouble."

"Sure," Spoons said. "Sure."

The big building felt cold. "Scared shit out of me," Spoons said. "Creekland must have been at chow."

Moultrie looked through a window back toward the guard. "Do you know that guy?"

"He's crazy. He's the one that snuck that shell into Two and blew half the lights out. Come on. It's downstairs. We take the elevator."

They got out and stood in a long hallway. A sign over the double doors read "Book Bindery."

"What now?" Spoons asked.

"We wait," Moultrie said, feeling more at ease now. The light was good here. They propped themselves against the double doors.

Moultrie was looking at his watch—"Couple of minutes yet"—when he heard the first noise from the corner. "Cat?"

But Spoons was already moving, groping, holding his knife. Crouched, he edged toward the shadowy boxes. He staggered back and fell as a box flew forward and hit him.

"Jesus Christ!"

A shape leapt from the shadows. A man from behind the boxes.

Moultrie grabbed for his knife—too late. His face stung and a blow to his shoulder knocked him to the floor. Jerking out his knife, he slashed at the form above him. The man gasped and staggered toward a staircase.

"You bastard!" he said, slowly backing up the steps into the dark. "You bastard!"

132

Moultrie lay on the floor, his face bleeding badly. "My God!" he said, holding his hand to his face, watching his palm fill with blood. "My God!"

Spoons was kneeling beside him. "Jesus Christ! Did he get you in the gut? Moultrie, good God! Did he get you bad?" Spoons began unbuttoning Moultrie's shirt.

"No, no—shoulder! Right shoulder. It's alright. My face, though. Oh, God, look at the blood!"

"Take it easy. It's not bad. Here's a handkerchief." Spoons pressed it to the side of his face.

"I got him once. I got the bastard a good one in the gut."

"We got to get out of here. He's still in here somewhere."

"Listen!" Moultrie said.

"What?"

"The elevator."

The elevator light was gleaming through the crack in the doors. Spoons spun around clawing the floor for his knife. "Can't find it!"

"Come on! Come on!" Moultrie whispered.

The doors opened. Beauchampes and Brown walked out.

Carefully, Moultrie rose. One hand clamped the handkerchief to his face, the other held his knife ready.

"What'd you try to pull?"

"What in hell happened to you?" Beauchampes asked.

"You blew it, brother," said Moultrie.

Beauchampes began raising his hands. "Take it easy, man. This ain't my style."

Moultrie motioned them over. "Frisk them, Spoons."

Spoons ran his hands over them. "Clean."

133

Holding his knife high, Moultrie glanced at the handkerchief soppy with blood. Beauchampes tensely adjusted his glasses. Brown did not move.

"Sloppy job. He must have used Bushaxe."

"What?" Moultrie said, his face beginning to burn.

"He should have got you first swipe. Sloppy work, man," Beauchampes said.

"Moultrie, maybe we should talk later," Spoons said.

"No! We talk now. What's the deal, Beauchampes? You in or not?"

Beauchampes lit a cigarette. "Looks like I have to be —now. That bullshit about two ounces pure—that wasn't too smart, you know?"

"So?"

"So what do we do now? You said you could run this party."

"I think we should hit back," Spoons said. "We let him know we're not chicken shit. Maybe we can parlay it out then. Bushman's his top man. We hit Bushman."

"Wrong," Moultrie said. "He cut me. Nobody does that." He paused to press the handkerchief hard to his cheek. "I've checked it out. He's got a pretty little screw boy. Calls her Kate. I say we hit Kate."

Beauchampes blew a couple of smoke rings. "Pretty tough."

"I don't know . . ."

"You shut up, Spoons. That bastard cut me, goddammit! Now, who do we get for the job?"

"There's a guy here—John Darcy," Beauchampes began.

"Black?" Moultrie asked.

"Yeah. They call him the angel of death. Uses an ice

pick—right through the ear. Any lock in the prison he can pick. At night, he slips right into the cell. You can never hear him, man. Smell him, though. You can smell that mother fifty yards away. His sides, guts are rotting out. Cancer, I guess. He always keeps a bundle of rags over it under his shirt. It seeps right through, though. It stinks like hell."

Moultrie looked at the handkerchief. The bleeding had almost stopped but he felt a little dizzy. "How do we get him?"

Beauchampes said that Darcy was the Muslim's man now. He said it was the way the Muslim really ran the prison, and that there was no one safe with Darcy and that he could get in anywhere. "The key is, he works for snow and the Muslim sells him just enough to get by. He needs it for the pain. You promise him a little *free* snow and he might do anything."

"Do it," Moultrie said.

Beauchampes smiled and pinched his cigarette behind his back. "You want to give me a little incentive, man?"

Moultrie thought quickly. "Alright. Two o'clock tomorrow you meet Spoons in his cell. He'll have money. You get word to Darcy. Tell him to come by my cell at six."

"Need more time."

"Three days, goddammit! No more!"

"Alright," Beauchampes said.

"Anything else?"

"You better take Brown here for a little protection. I got other boys. Things are going to get pretty rough around here."

Brown smiled.

135

"Okay," Moultrie said. "Now I got to figure how to get past the shakedown."

"Wash off most of that blood, then just follow me," Beauchampes said.

They found a tap and Moultrie wiped the obvious blood away. Creekland was standing at the shakedown spot. As they passed through the yellow circle, Beauchampes nodded at Creekland, who turned away. In the Yard, Beauchampes broke away, slipped into the Tunnel. Brown loped along behind Moultrie and Spoons.

"Maybe you shouldn't fool around with Darcy," Spoons said. "There's more to him than Beauchampes let on. It's like he doesn't even bother with locks. It's like he goes right through the walls. At night, nobody ever sees or hears him, even in the showers. Just smell him. There's something more to him, man."

"I hope so," Moultrie said, his face throbbing. "I hope to God he's death itself!"

18

BREEN had been to the post office and again no letter. During the last two years, the Provincial had let him know something by the first of October, anyway. *Probably given me a life sentence in this joint.* As he pushed open the double doors, the hot, rich odor of the infirmary rushed out and over him like a tarp. Medicines and bedpans and soiled linens and that peculiar smell, sweet and failing, that came from men who no longer struggled or fought for life.

The beds were neat and white and the sun, through the long windows, stood hard on them. Now and again, Breen stopped and talked to a man, taking down his name for a special intention at Mass or writing down the name and phone number of a mother or sister for a "vital" message.

"Hey, Father!"

"Morning, Matt. How's the foot?"

Matthew Wells sat on the edge of his bed in red flannel pajamas, one foot soaking in a tub.

"It's taking to soak in this here salt. Which is what I told them to do when I first got here. It tugs it right out— the poison. The salt sucks it right out like a catfish." He lifted up the foot which was white and swollen tightly about a deep cut. "It's them damn picks. They could keep them clean if they wanted to. It cut right through my foot and the lockjaw behind it." He squinted one eye shut and wiped a hand across his face.

"Did I tell you about the new appeal? Oh, yeah, my lawyer's got another one cooking. I shouldn't be in here anyway, you know. Got framed. Yeah, got screwed by the system."

Breen folded his hands behind his back and said that it was just too damn bad that so many innocent men were getting screwed and framed, particularly the guys in this prison. Both of them laughed, then. They talked for a time and Matthew Wells asked for a blessing and got one and Breen moved on.

He stopped at a chess game and tried to talk with the two men. They were dark Sicilians and did not say anything. Breen was talking about Ruy Lopez and pawn victories and the dangers of the four knights game and they said nothing. Breen said that Sunday was coming up and that maybe they'd like to get their asses to Mass once in a while. They fiddled with their sunglasses and lit up cigars.

"Hey, Father. Want to sign my cast?" a young boy called out four or five beds down.

138

"Sure," Breen said. He moved beside the bed and scribbled his name on the cast.

"I'm Catholic—kind of," the boy said, blushing, not looking at Breen.

"So am I," Breen said with a smile.

The boy's face brightened like a plate. "Once I was thinking about being a priest. Decided I couldn't make it."

"Why?"

"Did something real dumb and robbed a store one Wednesday night. Only got forty bucks."

"Better than me. I make a heist every Sunday in broad daylight and don't get half that."

The boy asked about the Blue team and Breen said that they were good, better than ever.

Finally, he came to Charlie Jenkins. "Morning, Charlie."

"Doing all right, Father."

Charlie Jenkins was rubbing one weak hand across his bald head. "Ole Bernace went today. About eleven, Doc said. Did you ever know him, Father—Bernace Campbell? Big ole boy with yellow hair?"

"I don't think so."

"The TB finally got him, I reckon."

"I'm sorry," Breen said.

"Oh, they'll tell you some bad tales on him, these ole boys around here, but he was good. Mighty good. We built that still together, you know. Good gracious, all them kids. They're going to miss that ole boy."

"Is there somebody to help out?"

"He's got kin. They'll all pitch in there. But you know, he could really suck the tunes out of a mouth harp, and spoons! Why, he could play spoons to make brick dance for the Devil's furnace." He was quiet a moment, recollecting.

"Maybe it was just as well that he passed on. He wasn't really happy since he lost his eye. He had one of them glass ones. I remember when a tall wind would come up, lots of times you'd see him sneak behind a tree so you couldn't watch and get all catty-cornered and pop it out. He'd spit on it a little bit, waller it around in his hanky and shove it back perty as you please." He laughed.

Breen saw beyond this though, to the grief which was now resting lightly and tight on his face and that hung in his eyes like a stone. He knew how it was for these hard men and that they would have grief out their own way.

"Moose Club gave it to him—that eye. They brought him up in front of all the Mooses—drunk, all of them eating baked beans and chicken salad, and right there between the American flag and the Moose banner gave it to him. It winked and danced in that little box and he was proud as a new penny and liked to 'a bawled over it." Jenkins slipped his hands to his face and wept.

Breen rubbed a hand behind his neck, coughed, shuffled his feet. "Charlie, look . . . don't cry. I mean, don't . . ." He felt the other men staring. Reached a hand out, then brought it back. *Why in hell didn't something come to him now when it was needed?* For a moment, he saw himself reaching through the glucose tubes, across the tray of pills and medicines, and holding Jenkins to his chest . . . but he could not. "You . . . you just got to tough it out, Jenkins. Look—he's dead and gone and you just got to gut it through. There's nothing else."

Breen was halfway down the stairs before the cool breeze from the Tunnel stopped him. "Damn!" he whispered, sticking his hands on his hips, shaking his head—then abruptly he spun to his right, slammed both fists into a wooden door. He slumped back against the wall. Wasn't it something, though? Twenty-five years a priest and all he could say was—tough it out, gut it through, buddy! He held his big hands in front of himself, the knuckles skinned, bleeding, clenching them in the light. Studying them a minute, he crammed them into his pockets. Twenty-five years and all he could do was coach football teams and beat the hell out of some scrawny, starry-eyed kid who told him he was born to be a cop.

"Yeah. I'm one hell of a guy," he said to himself. "Why in God's name didn't somebody make me bishop."

In the sacristy, beginning his vesting prayers. Slipping into the alb, smelling of incense and ashes. Tightening the cincture. At Mass, he tried to concentrate on the prayers, to lift up his heart. He could not. He only became irritated at the irregular working of the furnace or the mistake of a server or those who left early. Twenty minutes and it was over. Back in the sacristy, he folded the vestments neatly. With the stole, he made an M for Mary. Came out and knelt before the altar. Praying for all those who had asked him to. Trying to pray for White, but it did not go well. Then he prayed for himself, that he be given courage. He prayed for this because he was fifty now, and knew he could be little more than he was. Courage was good and bulky, unlike grace. Courage he could hold in his belly. It would stick to his ribs. It would see him through.

19

MOULTRIE was waiting in his cell at 5:45.

Most of the men had been fed. They lay in their cells, some already asleep. Outside the river was running dark and silent and the frost creeping through the big rocks by the river and laying hold to the bars here. Sealing the windows, rending the dark stones farther apart. The night wind gathered and grew in the north.

Spoons was late. Rising from his bunk, Moultrie took a long drink from the tap. The water was cold and he sat back down remembering a time when he was young— those dusty yellow afternoons when he waited, high in the attic, to speak with his father. Only one door separated the boy from his father and the bodies of the dead. Though the keyhole was filled with tissue, the boy could still smell them. At two o'clock his father came out.

Break time. His white shirt was opened at the middle of his chest and rolled neatly up his forearms. They sat by the summer window, the wind blowing sun and dust and the sweetness of the trees. They listened to the dark crickets. His father said the crickets tried to spark a fire with their legs and cook the kernels of grass, for they were hungry. The boy said yes, though not really believing him, for he was too big for such tales now. The boy talked to his father about school, about his ideas, and a speech he was to make. His father laughed in his big way and hugged him. Told the boy that he was smart, and the boy rejoiced. They drank water then from a stone jar. The father went first, tilting back his beautiful neck and drinking long and silent. Then the boy. The water tasted cold and sweet. Small stones lay in the bottom of the jar. His father put them there because he said they brought sweetness to the water. A little while longer they talked, but the scent of embalming fluid from the father's shirt made the boy's eyes weep. Seeing this, the father kissed him on the cheek and passed back into the room of the dead. . . .

"Moultrie! Moultrie, goddammit!" Spoons was shaking him. "Here's the stuff. Come on, he'll be here soon."

"How much did you get?"

"Beauchampes said it would keep him three, four days. You sure you want to go through with this?"

Moultrie touched the still-fresh cut on his face. "I'm sure."

"I tell you there's something more to this guy. You got a knife?"

"Yes."

"I'll be in my cell. If something happens—I'm only

143

thirty feet away." Spoons considered him a moment, then disappeared down the tier.

The chapel bells were tolling six o'clock. Some men began showers. Moultrie could hear them singing in the darkness. In the darkness their voices sounded soft and round. Moultrie was barely breathing, but even so, he thought he could smell something. Creeping by the cell door. Hear something, too, a sound like leaves, soft, restless. And slowly the odor and the sound were growing as if to fill the whole building. No longer could he hear the men singing. Guardedly, he rose from the bunk, looking out on the tier. Empty. It was when he eased outside the cell, staring into the dark, that something scuttled across his feet and scrambled up his trousers. Slapping at his legs, he stumbled back into his cell where he saw his trousers swarming with roaches. Even the walls and floor were glittering with their flashing backs as they flew into his hair and eyes.

On the first floor, the guards were spraying insecticide. Moultrie could hear the laughter and picture them watching the roaches stream toward the ceiling and darken the lights. On his bunk, he wrapped himself in a blanket. He lay still for some minutes. Occasionally a roach wiggled under the blanket and he would crush it, at the same time tugging the blanket tightly around him. Gradually the rustling faded away. He shook the blanket. Felt no movement. Cautiously, he peeped out. The room seemed free. He looked around the cell, wondered if he was going crazy. Then, from the tier, a soft voice whispered, "Moultrie." He waited. Had he heard his name? He saw nothing.

"Moultrie?"

"Is that you, Darcy?"

"Yes."

"Come into the light where I can see you."

John Darcy limped into the cell. Thin as brown wrapping paper. His eyes veiled in gray at the pupils and sunken in gray and dark sockets, looking like goggles about his face. His chin frail, almost transparent. There was a deep, strange smell.

"A brother told me that—you and me, we might make ourselves a little deal." Darcy was pulling his coat over what seemed to be a large bundle in his left side.

"They say," Moultrie said, his heart wild in his chest, "that with an ice pick you're pretty good."

Darcy pulled at one sock. "They call me 'the angel of death.' I like that. Maybe I am."

Moultrie waited for something more, a grin or a cackle. None came.

Darcy scratched behind one ear. Flakes scattered down the front of his coat and onto the floor. "It is the soap which causes this," he said. "They should put oil in it. It is bad soap. Many men are afflicted."

Moultrie felt his stomach grab. Easily, he sat down on the bunk. "I need a hit made, and I need somebody to stay with me on a long-term deal."

"The hit I can do."

"You work for me alone, or forget it."

"Then we forget it, brother."

Moultrie took the package of cocaine from under his pillow. "The Muslim's out. Any time I want to, I can stop your stuff or anybody else's. Or—I can get you more, cheaper."

"Grand words," Darcy said, barely audible.

Moultrie handed him the package. "Open it up. That's what we're talking about. That's what I can give you."

"The Muslim gives nothing. I pay, and too much." Darcy opened the package and leaned into it.

"That's a little present."

Darcy looked up.

"Work for me."

"Such snow—it is so cool and good."

"You got to be with me as long as I need you."

Darcy tasted the cocaine. Sucked his finger and wiped it against his trousers. "Who is it and when?"

"It's the kid he screws, do you know him?"

"Calls her Kate. He's kept her two years now."

"Will it be hard?"

"Not in this building. Do you know how it works? Right through the ear. You only go so far. There is the secret. Too much blood otherwise. If you do it just right, you can clean them up with the corner of a cotton handkerchief. I will show you." Darcy took out two oranges from his coat pocket and held them in one hand. "I practice well and often." In the other hand he held an eight-inch ice pick. "You go clear through one, then just through the skin of the other. You never bruise the flesh of the other—it is too much. Watch."

In an instant the ice pick flashed into the oranges. Darcy gave the second orange to Moultrie. Juice was running down his arm. "You look and see."

Moultrie pulled the peel back. The flesh had not been pierced. He shuddered, but did not let Darcy see. "It's good," he said.

"There's a popping when it goes through the ear. It is easier than oranges. You learn to—feel it."

146

"I need this done quick," Moultrie said.

"Tonight? I could do it tonight if you want."

"That's good. Do it tonight, then."

Outside, in the killing zone, a dog howled.

Darcy cringed, holding the ice pick tightly. "I hate dogs," he slurred. "I would kill every one if I could. Look what they done to me." He pulled up his pants leg. Half of the calf muscle was missing.

"Christ, how did that happen?"

"They sicced one on me when I was little. It drug me around the yard. It liked to 'a killed me." Darcy stared at his calf for a moment, then carefully pulled the pants leg down. He slipped out the door. "Two days—I get back to you."

"Good," Moultrie said. There was only darkness. He sat down on the bunk and tried to think it over. The cell smelled of Darcy.

"How'd it go? I heard part of it. What happened?" Spoons asked, peering into the cell.

"Tonight he hits Kate."

For an instant Spoons was stunned, then he slapped his fist into his hand. "I don't believe it. We've done it. We've got them all behind us." He quickly sobered. "But we have to watch. Like Beauchampes said—it's going to get rough. The Muslim's got two, maybe three bodyguards. We better have at least that many."

"Yeah," Moultrie said quietly. "Yeah, we'll do that. Let's get to supper. Find Brown."

"We can't go to the cafeteria tonight. Are you crazy?"

"It's in the open the way you like it. Lots of people." Moultrie put on a jacket. He felt cold.

"If the Muslim finds out about this hit, he might be

147

mad or scared enough to do something stupid out there."

"We're going, goddammit! We face what we are."

They went to supper. Moultrie ate little. Brown watched his back. Moultrie did not see the Muslim. Later, back in his cell, he felt a little guilty and frightened—not because of what he had done, but because the act gave him a strange kind of pleasure, negotiating the death of a man he had never seen. He wondered at this and questioned himself long into the night, feeling a cold awakening and dread.

Throughout the night, he thought he heard John Darcy, the steps as soft as soot rising and falling in darkness. The terrible mangled leg setting itself down in a fine and delicate cadence. But each time he raised his head, he saw only shadows and the lights of the cell block. Near dawn he drifted to sleep.

While Moultrie and all slept, in the prison's deepest dark, John Darcy stalked ruined in the night. He slipped down from the fourth tier. With deaf ears all heard the handrail squeal and whistle like a last warning as death descended to cell 116, where Kate lay in sweet and pudgy slumber. She was naked, just sweating in a weak brine that the Muslim had come to cherish these two years. Along with the ticking of her clock, which grew weaker and farther away, was another sound—a ticking, too, the lock opening like a heart in good rhythm.

The door, fearfully betraying, hushes itself wide, and she, in dreamful disdain, turns her soft body to the wall. As quick as light—once and no more—through her ear comes a shudder and a falling away from these dreams, a piling down and rendering to darkness. And the last of all things to Kate is cotton, soft and swirling in her ear.

148

TWO

I

LINIMENT and the hot showers and the block of
chalk, white and dry, that the weight lifter had used on
his hands.

"You look real—strong," Childs said, shaking in front
of his first regular.

Pace MacIntosh sucked in his slight belly, cocking his
shoulders back, rubbing talcum powder over his hairless
chest. "Worked hard at it. Squats and bench presses.
Using weight to make weight." His eyes cut down Childs,
who managed to scour a towel across his legs just outside
the showers. "You got pretty good cuts yourself. You
lift?"

"No," Childs said.

MacIntosh rubbed nervously behind one ear. "I don't
do this often, you know. Just once in a while." He looked

151

at Childs sternly, pointing a finger. "I'm no fag, buddy. A guy just gets a little horny in here. All over my cell, I got pictures of my wife and"—he was holding up three fingers, fanning them with his left thumb—"three kids."

"Do I take off all my clothes with you?"

MacIntosh smiled, scratching at his dimpled chin. "Pretty green, huh? Don't worry, old Pace will break you in easy."

So in the past few days he had gone to bed with Pace MacIntosh and three others since him. With two of them he was so afraid he vomited and they became angry, but got their money's worth anyway. The first night he was frightened, not having understood what Montana meant by paying him back, and he was going to leave until Red reminded him that Stuckey was still out there. Still waiting for him. Then he gave over and Red took him to bed, helped prepare him for the regulars. Montana was very gentle and the next day began teaching Childs about lubricants, lotions, positions, methods of easing soreness, vitamins. And all these lessons seemed to help Childs deal with the terror and guilt he felt at his first encounters. Though there was one night when he cried and hated himself, feeling as if some division had taken place, some final loss. But Montana, nuzzling his ear, had told him a simple, dark, comforting thing: "If we're made to do these things, baby—forced to love men instead of women—we ain't going to be damned for it. We didn't choose all this. Besides, here there is no other way." In himself Childs was not sure of Montana's thinking, and for a while he was in despair because the lights would not come to him. But after a while his despair turned to anger against the lights for having left him. After all,

152

like Montana said, he had not chosen this way. So now he did not bother to call the lights anymore. He did not need them.

Coming to in the morning: ringing Count bells, clanging iron, the deep, throaty barking of sleepy men, blaring radios; the dim cell filled with frilly things, doilies darned on the window bars, paper flowers against the walls; stuffed animals; powders and ointments and perfumes, the dark sharpness of the commode. Feeling the fine dirt of the cell under his feet, he splashed cold water on his face at the basin, took a towel and turned to see Montana lying in his bunk. Smeared with pungent ointments, skewered by a rectal thermometer, reading his cross-referencing medical dictionaries.

"I think I could wear two," Childs said, gazing back into the mirror at the rhinestone in his ear.

Montana tugged from a laxative bottle, wiped his mouth on a handkerchief.

"Rose is the only one who has done that."

"Why her?"

"Take this thing out, will you?"

Childs removed the thermometer, glanced at it, and put it in the sink.

"Well?"

"Safe," Childs said, parting his hair in the middle.

Montana sighed. His face became soft and long. "She was the most beautiful man in this prison. Listen, honey, thirty-five years ago guys were dueling over her favors with all they had. Once in a while some guy still sends her roses from outside."

Childs was sliding into his jeans, clean blue work shirt.

"Maybe you should stay in tonight. Things are getting

153

too tight in this place. This guy Moultrie—he's a fool. They say he killed Kate. She was a bitch and I don't miss her, but she was the Muslim's."

"The movie will be over early."

"Yeah, I'm probably just a little jumpy. Go ahead and get your tricks over for this week. Rest up."

Childs nodded, moving toward the door.

Montana rose from the bunk and handed Childs one of the movie passes. "Who is it you're meeting tonight?"

"Pickup. You just said to sit by the third window."

"Oh, yeah," Montana said. "I forgot." He stroked Childs's face. "You got any idea how many boys I got working for me?"

Childs shook his head.

"Forty, and not one of them pretty as you. They know it too, baby. They're jealous. If you started choosing, they know you could have anybody you want. But you won't do that to Montana, will you?"

Childs felt Montana wanted some kind of promise, but he was learning now not to make promises. "I got to go."

Red dropped his eyes. "Sure. Go ahead, Danny. Just be cool. Just remember who—loves you."

Moving down through the tiers past Naiobi Johnson's cell, which smelled clean, bright, of fresh ironing. As if some piece of sun hung in the corner while Naiobi Johnson ironed all day and all night. Seeing Naiobi standing white and tiny and frail like china, but wheeling the huge dazzling iron as he had for twenty years, careful not to fall off his apple crate. Past Tom Parham's cell, walls entirely covered with baseball cards, a treasury of gum said to be beneath the floor. Past Matthew Forb's cell, the nigger who weighed four hundred pounds, his

154

big sides lapping at the walls. Everything covered and stained by semen, all he ever did. The whole tier smelling dully of it. Past Marly Perkins' cell: the guards allowed him to light all of his candles once briefly every night. And how his room glittered like the sky then, casting spells across his many statues and crosses.

Searched at the building gate. Out into the Tunnel. Searched at the entrance to the cafeteria. Just before going in, he saw John Hawkins across the Tunnel. For a second they surveyed one another's faces across the distance, then Hawkins turned back toward the cell blocks. Slipping into the candy-wrapper noise of the cafeteria, Childs let the darkness cover the shame he felt, sat down by the third window. Waiting.

Trying to forget about Hawkins, he wondered who was about to meet him and what he would be like, and he was surprised to find that much of the fear had left him, replaced with a kind of excitement. Smelling sweat and popcorn, drinks, candy, the different clothes: wool, cotton, nylon. And packed about him deodorants, perfumes and laughter and shouting and anger, and he waded into all of it as though it were a good, muddy, silt June river.

At last the movie begins and the men applaud and bellow, then become quiet. And Childs can hear the rattle of the guards' key chains, see their cigarettes flare and fade like signals in the dark. Feeling a hand on his leg now, a closeness and pulse. And in the cafeteria, the darkness has a heart which races as wildly as his own.

2

"No guns. There's laws that have to be kept here. No hardware."

"Guns scare people. I want the Muslim and his people scared."

"The screws will find out. As soon as you get them, they'll know," Spoons said.

"A couple thirty-eights is all. Beauchampes says he can get them in on the dairy truck. Brothers at the farm will seal them in plastic bags, then stuff them in a barrel of cottage cheese. Not bad, huh?"

"Just stupid."

"Listen, if I had to, I'd smuggle a keg of TNT into this place to blow the Muslim out. I'm not interested in this law or balance you keep talking about. There's one thing I want—to bring the Muslim down!"

Moultrie and Spoons were waiting in the upper ward

of Building Three for Rayfield Jones, who was to show Moultrie part of his whiskey operation.

Jones came up the stairwell from the Tunnel. He was a tall, broad-shouldered man of about sixty. He and Moultrie shook hands. Moultrie had not seen him for a month, since Jones first swung his support to the plan.

At the back of the ward, in the lavatory, Moultrie was introduced to Jones's four sons. According to Jones, the family had made whiskey on the outside for a long time, but when he got busted he found the money was better here, so he had his boys commit minor offenses and brought them in for a year or two. "Kind of like the service," he said, smiling. "But each one of those younguns has got his own new house and wife and kids. And they be set up good when they get out."

Moultrie looked at the boys. The oldest one seemed about twenty-three. All of them were shy, kept their eyes to the floor. So that Moultrie wanted to hold them in his arms and ask them did they know who they were. That more than any other being they were of this earth, imbued with all its fire and genius and motion, and that they did not have to look away from any man. And that the time was coming when their youth must sweep the white mold from the earth, scrape the mildew from the good black soil.

Jones said then that a few of the Muslim's men had come around just after Kate's death trying to pressure him. He had spit in their faces. Told them he was a God-fearing Baptist and had hated the Muslim from the beginning.

"But he's a mean man," Jones said. "You watch yourself, son."

Moultrie smiled. "Tell me about your operation."

157

Nine stools, one of them with its top down. Jones ran his hand across it. "We got one john working for us in every bathroom. Throw a few potatoes and yeast in the top, runs right down to the bowl through all that nice copper tubing. Best cooker a man could have. We change johns every couple days when we get a new load of buck. You want a taste?"

Moultrie eyed the stools. "Well . . . sure."

They all laughed and Moultrie thought that maybe what Spoons had said about taking whiskey away was right. A lot of men abused it on the outside, but here, maybe they really needed it. A wooden ladle came round to him. The whiskey went down smoother than he thought it would. "Good," he said. "Good and clean." He wiped his mouth, handed back the ladle. "Don't the screws do something about all this?"

Jones propped the small of his back with his flat, black hands. "Not for a few gallons a week they don't. Sometimes though, sometimes they get edgy. Bust up a few of these beauties. Tore up a couple last week. Something's bothering them. Makes me a little nervous when they start doing stupid things. Means trouble. But that's the time the fruit comes in handy."

Spoons poked Moultrie in the ribs. "Get hold of this one."

"Matthew, my youngest. It was his idea. Takes a hypodermic, shoots up an orange or apple with that clear whiskey. Times like this, it's better than selling cups or jars from the wards. Oh, the screws know about the fruit, too. But it's not so open. They don't feel like they really have to do something."

Moultrie laid his hands on Jones's shoulders. "You

158

built this business, these boys, good and strong. If there's more trouble with the Muslim, you let me know."

"One thing about the Muslim," Jones said, gazing at Moultrie intently. "He won't quit. Not till it's finally over. You know that?"

"No more blood. We talk it out now," Moultrie said.

"No," Jones said firmly.

Moultrie raised his chin, questioning.

"He's going to end you. You killed his lover and made it personal. You cut into his heart and he'll end you for it."

Something rising in the light of Jones's eyes made Moultrie shudder. And for the first time since he was a boy, when he cried and called out in the bitter, howling nights, helpless and alone, did he feel the old fear against his spine like some frozen pit of sleep: that any act on his part was hopeless, that something was seeking him out, ravenous and consuming.

All the way back to the cell he was shivering—questions, questions scattering through his head like leaves. Carefully, he hung up his shirt and placed his shoes exactly beside the other pairs. Sitting down on the bunk, he slowly repeated to himself that all was well. There was nothing to fear. He stretched out on the bunk and tried to laugh. He was strong and well and must not analyze himself so. He made the old fear lie down in himself, covering it with many things: pictures, memories, the sure and ordered workings of the past, when . . . when he was first thrown into prison in Charleston. When he stood on the platform and his people screamed his name and he, by a slow turning of his head and eyes, silenced them all. Or, with a sweep of his hand and rage in his

159

voice, hurled them into anger and brought their sleeping souls to life. And when the police came and locked him up, he remembered his brothers storming through the streets, chanting: "Moses! Moses! Moses!" And waiting in the molding cell by the street where the white man beat him in the face, his mouth pouring blood. And when they left how he cupped his hands letting them fill with blood and stuck them out the bars and the great silence falling upon his people as they dipped their fingers and handkerchiefs and babies' fingers into his blood. . . .

3

"MOVE closer to the bars."

"They don't usually do this with me, son."

"Rules. I just follow them."

His back to the Tunnel, Breen pressed against the cold bars. Saw the cameras panning back and forth near the ceiling of the hall.

Stepping back into the blinking new control room, the guard pressed a button. The gate to the mental ward slid open.

About two o'clock the day before, Jesse Cates, a young man—tough, quick, not easily jarred—had come to see Breen. The Warden wanted Breen to check out a rumor that Joseph Valànce knew something about . . . a little trouble brewing. Cates said that Valànce had been asking to see a priest for some time anyway and that they didn't pass the word along because—well, hell, he was crazier than a bedbug, already killed something like eleven people. Grinning then, the Warden abruptly changed the subject, throwing up his fists, and said that Breen must have one hell of a punch and that he never knew priests were allowed to have at it and he hoped that little bantam rooster did better if something went wrong in this place. The remark irritated Breen. White was an idiot, but he had guts. The Warden had no place in their quarrel. Breen brushed the remark aside and said he would see this Valànce, report back any information that didn't fall under the mantle of confession.

"Piss is the main thing," the guard was saying. "The kitchen crew, they sneak cups into him and he throws it all over you. You ever get piss in your mouth?"

"I'll be going on down," Breen said.

"You need help, call out or wave. I'll see it on the screen."

The long hall was brightly lit. An orderly let Breen through two gates. Took him to cell number seven. Outside the cell, a wall camera coldly observed all. Valànce was sitting on his bunk—a lumbering red body in the white cell.

"You the priest?"

"That's right."

"That collar suppose to convince me?"

"You tell me."

"I used a collar a couple times."

"Have fun?"

"You afraid to be here?"

"Scared shitless."

"Sit down in that chair."

Breen sensed a terrible strangeness here. Sitting down, he made all of his movements open and slow.

Valànce's black eyes gleamed like beetles. "They tell

162

me you speak Portuguese. Been to Brazil. You ever seen a town called Carota?"

"No."

"It's in the mountains. Ninety-eight hundred feet above sea level."

"What's all this crap about trouble? Somebody planning some trouble?"

Valànce grinned. "I thought that would get you here. But it's true. Trouble—I can feel it coming. Get a pain right back here." He touched the back of his head. "In Alcatraz when it blew, I got blackjacked. Ever since then, when my head hurts I know. Besides, I've been hearing things from the kitchen crew." Valànce bent over, pulling a box from under his bunk.

A clanking brought Breen's eyes to Valànce's feet where a double-banded leg iron and heavy chain gripped his ankle, stained with iodine. The chain was fastened beneath the bed to a wall.

"These books I read say there was an earthquake there in fifty-seven or fifty-six. Subcontinental shelf shifted. The Rema fault."

Breen folded his arms. Waiting. The cell felt unusually cold.

"According to this map, there's a dam right here." He held up a map of southern Brazil, pointing to a black circle just above the town. "Fifty pounds of dynamite and I figure she'll go up real good."

"Why not a hundred?" Breen snapped.

"On the way over, I'll get the bacteria, slip it into the feed. Animals, domestic animals, die in six to ten minutes depending on humidity, heat. After the flood, I figure the people will eat whatever meat they can find. Humans take a little longer to die. Humans take about twelve minutes to cough up their guts. Got something to say about all this?"

"They tell me you murdered eleven people."

"Closer to twenty." Valànce picked up his leg chain, rolling it in his hands.

"What do you do, notch them on your chain?" Breen said strongly.

"Stephen Vincent Benét. You read him? I do. Once I was reading him to a third grader out in a mess of honeysuckle. Beat his brains out with a big rock. Couldn't recognize him afterwards. Another time I—"

"Shut up!" Breen said, his fists clenching.

Valànce's face paled. He stuck his fingers into his hair, a black grin streaming across his lips. "You just think I'm crazy like the rest of them. You're wrong. What I do has a reason, just like the stars. There have to be murderers. They're in the plan. I was born, conceived before all time to hate. I am hate. I'd kill you if I could. When I came here, I'd already killed a lot of people. Got four more serving time. What do I care? I'll get another one before long. Maybe that orderly. They could give me the chair, but they won't. They should, but they're too stupid to see it. I'd like to strangle you all. I'd like to chew the marrow out of your bones."

Breen slowly rose from his seat. "I think you're a bluffer, a talker, Valànce."

"A man has to . . . to communicate. Has to reveal his soul to another man once in a while. 'Confession is good for the soul'? It keeps us from the beasts. And I am human, priest. I'm in the plan as much as you, and that's what you are all afraid of."

Breen looked into his eyes at a deep and burrowing

164

darkness. Knowing that here again he could give no help, though he felt the slightest pleading, infinite and minute, as if only one cell out of billions still held fiercely to light, though all the rest were blind with darkness.

The cameras whirred along the walls. The electric gates opened and closed. Breen felt a lessening: despair; anger. Knowing that not even in the prayers of Mass could there be hope here. *And maybe there was never supposed to be. Maybe Valànce was right. Maybe before all time he and every man was. . . .* But he shut these thoughts down, stowed them back deeply into himself.

"Get any on you?" the guard asked, grinning beneath the buzzing neon lights.

Ten o'clock at night in the rectory, and Breen stood at the foot of the stairs where the candles fluttered yellow before the chipped statue of Mary. Beneath her feet lay the serpent, mouth agape, wide and yawning. Adjusting the lace tablecloth freshly ironed by Naiobi Johnson, Breen said a small prayer above the candles and let it go easily into the great dark night—for peace and submission, acceptance. For all here a long-limbed and cool peace. Up the stairs, going past White's room, he felt a draft. *Never thinks about the heating bill.* He knocked on the door. No answer. "White?"

Some days before White had asked for his key and begun locking himself in his room two or three nights a week. He had grown thinner and always seemed tired.

With his passkey, Breen opened the door. The floor lay strewn with clothes. A guitar, music books, records— the wide-open window. Peering down into the courtyard between the gym and the rectory, Breen smelled the soft scent of cologne.

4

"Got him in the throat a couple of times. Hell of a mess."

"Peterson?" Walsh said again.

"Molester," Cays said quietly. "Had to happen."

"My God."

"Put a dummy in his bunk. Dropped the body down the elevator shaft. We didn't miss him in Count for a couple days."

For the next few hours Walsh was stunned. Blamed himself. He had wanted to help Peterson, had intended going to the Warden, but there had been the fight and the last two weeks just slipped away. Now he wondered if Rhiner was right about him. He and Rhiner—maybe they *were* the same animal. No real difference between them. Rhiner had done nothing deliberately. He himself had waited too long, and Peterson had been murdered as he said he would.

166

As the guilt began to wear down in himself, Walsh began to see the prison, feel it, as never before. He had not killed Peterson, nor had Rhiner. It was the system, and the system would fail again when the time for a formal investigation arrived. Not doing or waiting. Waiting or not doing. So he found his balance, decided how to move.

Cays was checking passes at the Tunnel door when Walsh pulled him aside.

"How do you dial information around here?"

"About what?" Cays asked.

"Anything, everything."

"Peterson, you mean."

Walsh didn't answer.

"You should stay out of this, you know?"

Walsh remained silent.

Cays shook his head, pushed his hat back. "Cally Derick at the truck pit. He's got a runner named Owens who knows most everything. But Derick's half nuts. You watch yourself, kid. You . . ." but Walsh was already headed through the Yard toward the truck pit, which lay on the outside wall of the Industry Building. Moving toward Officer Cally Derick, who was balancing on two legs of his chair, a pencil behind his ear, feet clad in white socks propped up on his desk. Wearing a green cap and glasses, his face like old yellow cracked dough.

"What you want from Owens?"

"A little information," Walsh said.

"About what?"

"Peterson," Walsh said, standing in warm sunlight, gazing at Derick through the doorway.

"The new sticking, huh?" Derick stared at him a moment, yanked off his glasses, held them against his belly, and laughed.

"He wants to know about that molester, Bo," Derick said to the enormous black man behind him who was ironing a shirt.

Bo-dick raised his huge head up from the ironing board, slobbering a bit, grinning, then his face fell back to the work.

Derick wiped some moisture from his eyes, tiny and gray, threatening like blisters. Settled his glasses back on the hawk-billed nose. "Well, come on in here, young man."

The truck maintenance office: crammed with fan belts, radiator caps, spark plugs, the giant black whose saliva drooled hissing on the iron, and in one corner a large, stinking green parrot, clacking its bill, rattling its black tongue against its beak.

Derick cocked his eyes shrewdly. "So they ain't forgot me in there. In the buildings they know ole Cally still remembers how to kick over the honey bucket, huh?"

"Maybe so," Walsh said.

Derick considered the remark a moment. "Owens ain't back yet. Gone to Spanish lab," he said, pulling his feet from the desk, slipping to the edge of his chair and cupping his hands over his ears, wiggling the fingers. "Wears them headphones. Learning Spic in Building One. I got no idea why."

Walsh took off his hat, held it in his hand.

"Owens—he's crazy but he's got good ears," said Derick, opening the door to a small, rusting refrigerator which was humming in the corner.

From inside the refrigerator, sharp, bitter odor of black earth seeped into the air.

"So I heard," Walsh said, pulling back his head from Derick's outstretched, earth-covered palm. The fat earthworm, red and glistening.

Winking, Derick pressed his finger to his lips. Clapping both hands behind his back, he began strutting in a stylized gait before the twitching parrot. "Mr. Tumblers, what say you, sir?"

"Hang the buggers, captain! Hang the buggers!" squawked the parrot.

Derick hunched halfway around, flashing a sly smile at Walsh, who sat determined to see Owens.

Bo-dick wiped sweat from his face and grinned.

Again Derick began pacing up and down before the parrot, which was ruffling its faded feathers, wagging its black tongue, tapping up and down the perch in exact rhythm with Derick, who was chanting now in his high wrenching voice. "Mr. Tumblers of late I've found, some black boys drank me whiskeys down."

"Drank 'em down, drank 'em down!" screamed the parrot.

Baring his teeth, Derick shot a look at Bo-dick, then turned and stuck his face directly into the parrot's. "Mr. Tumblers, of late I heard that black boys figger, don't keep their word. And if it's true a liar figgers, how's a man to save his jiggers?"

Screamed the bird: "Hang the niggers! Hang the niggers!"

Whipping his arm like a pitcher, Derick tossed the worm to the shrieking bird and raced howling over to Walsh, pointing back at the parrot, holding his sides, his thin voice screeching like gears. Walsh pretended to laugh. Pushed back the impulse to run for the door.

Still giggling, Derick wheezed and hacked his way

169

back to his desk. Balancing again in his chair, he sandwiched his hands between his thighs, shutting his eyes tight, then popping them open, still grinning a little. "Well, it's like I said, this Owens, he's a crazy one, you know. Oh, hell yeah. Always thinks he's got a meeting with the President. Every day."

"But you can still—kick over the honey bucket, right?"

Derick's face was spreading in delight. "That I can do. That I purely can. Why, if they had kept me over there in the buildings, we wouldn't be having all this trouble now." He glanced out the office window. "As it is, I'm glad as hell to be out of that hornet's nest now. Feels like it did in fifty-seven."

"Will you help or not?" Walsh asked, trying to sound strong. Convincing.

"We play us a little game here. It's fun, fun. We'll do it through the game. Using the tucker telephone."

"And what the hell is that?" Walsh was about to ask when, stepping through the doorway, thin, frying-pan black with drooping ears, arrived Tommie Owens. "Hey, bossman," he said to Derick, his eyes sliding over to Walsh.

Derick's face went cold. "Sit down."

Owens bashfully squatted down on a box, clipping his knees together, batting his eyes at Derick. "It ain't starting again today is it, boss? We ain't playing again so soon, is we?"

Walsh sensed a sickness here. Something which made his stomach grab. He looked again toward the door.

Derick rose, moving over to Bo-dick.

"Oh no," Owens sighed. "Oh me."

"You know what, Bo-dick?" Derick was churning his jowls around and screwing and unscrewing his eyes, leaning right into Bo-dick's face, puffing hard from his little round belly, his hands scratching up and down the small of his back like shuttles. "He's done it again, Owens over there. He's done called your mama a no-good nigger bitch who sired you off a mule."

Bo-dick's mouth slung down to his chest, the orange acorn eyes beating hard at Owens. "He done that again?"

"That boy right over there, you listening to me?" Derick slapped the huge, black face and the big head slopped to one side. "You hear me? You hear what I said, Bo-dick? That Owens just don't learn. Bad-mouthing the dead again."

Owens' thin face began to squirm, his jaws packing themselves together as he clamped both hands over his ears, grinding his feet into the floor.

Gulping down enormous lungfuls of air, Bo-dick shuffles toward Owens, his wide, grappling hands opening and closing, while Derick scampers behind whining: "Called your mama a whore. Go get him, Bo-dick. Don't you let that boy say them bad things about the blessed dead in Jesus!"

Bo-dick grabs Owens by the neck with one hand, the other closing about both calves. "What you done said, Owens?" he pants, pulling the boy close to his eyes. " 'Bout my mama, what you done said?"

"I ain't said nothing. You let me down, nigger! Get your hands off me!" screams Owens, his face savage and wild.

Derick tiptoes to a chair, pointing to it. "Come on,

Bo-dick. Don't you let that boy sass you. Don't you let that boy piss on your sweet mama's grave!"

Dragging Owens by one leg and the neck, Bo-dick throws him into the chair. Pins him tightly to the back. "You pissing on my mama's grave, Owens? What you done said? Huh? What you done now?"

Derick strips off Owens' left shoe and sock, saying: "He's whispering something, Bo-dick. Nastiness! I wish you would listen at them ugly-assed ole words!"

"Hold off," Walsh says, unsure of himself, coming to his feet.

Sweat pouring down his neck, Owens starts to scream but Bo-dick closes off his throat with one hand. "You better stop that whispering 'bout Mama. What you done said, Owens?"

Derick opens a trunk beside the chair, carefully pulling out the dusty box of the old field telephone, attaching the wire to Owens' naked ankle. He turns to Walsh. "Alright, ask away, young man."

Walsh is confused for a moment, trembling. "Tell me—tell me . . . about Peterson, the sticking."

Owens' face shining sweat, eyes frantically rolling about the sockets, his foot trying to scrape the wire away. Piping: "I don't know nothing! I don't know, please, please!"

"You know something. Say it. Tell me, Owens, or I'll crank up this phone," Walsh says, now surprised to find his own hand sliding across the smooth wood case.

Owens' eyes pump like pistons from his head. "I got to see the President! Today I got a meeting with the President! Please, please!"

172

Derick: "Get him now, Bo-dick, come on. Pissing right on her grave. I can see it. Come on now. . . ."

The parrot clacking its beak, wagging its tongue: "Hang the niggers! Hang the niggers!"

Bo-dick: "What you doing now, Owens, huh?"

And Walsh, too, suddenly finds himself screaming, catching the crank handle: "You sonofabitch! Who did the sticking? Who killed Peterson? Tell me, you bastard! Say it! Say it, goddamn you!"

And now, not far away, down the tracks beside the truck pit, like the subtle ring of first frost in the air or the snap of first November wind, there comes a thin, tenuous whistling, a faint moaning which hums through the rails and air. And all at once—they cease. Derick releasing Owens' foot; Bo-dick's long, pouting jaw receding. And silently the three approach the back window of the office, gazing at the tracks through barbed wire, mesmerized by the growing thunder and whistling as if by a spell, even the parrot quiet. Waiting. And Walsh, feeling a whirring in his palms, is shocked to see the crank being ground by his right hand and drops the "tucker telephone." While the great racing train wails along the tracks, blowing dirt like a storm, dragging its long chain of cars in a swinging, metric, steel cadence that makes the red earth and pines and the walls of this prison shake and quail like lesser souls before a huge presence in the night.

Hearing the trio whispering to one another before the window, feeling the rumble of the passing cars, Walsh stumbled out the door into the dazed afternoon light.

5

"WELL?" Montana Red was rubbing cold cream from his face. "Are you coming or not?"

"I don't know," Childs said.

Red fastened his eyes on Childs. He slugged down a handful of vitamins, chased them with water. "Oh, you know, baby."

Childs did not understand Montana's mood. For the past week he had been working hard for Red. Going out almost every night. He had even made a few friends among the regulars.

"This place won't keep secrets. The bars, the locks—they spread tales. They tell little stories. And I heard you've got yourself a few beaus now. Getting real popular."

"That ain't so. I been working. Paying you back."

Montana gave a bitter grin, then hurriedly dashed on

174

some mascara, glancing in the mirror. "Don't think you couldn't end up in the basement of the laundry like this little snip of a troublemaker we're going to visit. I want you to see him. Understand what happens to pretty boys who forget about their friends. See you there!" Red whirled around and left the cell, trailing perfume.

Childs got through the building and Yard doors easily. Red had given him one of the green permanent passes usually reserved for runners or trusties. So far the guards had never questioned him.

The laundry lay inside the Industry Building. In the past Childs had been there several times to try and explain to Hawkins what had happened. He felt a vague need for contact with the hazy world of his past—a need to talk to Hawkins—but as yet he had not. The windows of the laundry had been nailed over in plywood to keep out the cold river wind. As Childs moved through the building's dimness, the third shift climbed out of the washing vats and went toward the Cage, which was made of glass and built into one corner of the building. The glass helped to keep out the noise of the wringer and the odor of unwashed clothes during mealtime. It allowed the prisoners to be watched by the guards who were patrolling on catwalks overhead. Inside the Cage, the third shift winced, blinked, coming out of vats into bright light. The big overhead lamps helped the guards to watch the men while they ate. Over the years, some of the prisoners had put plants here because of the strong lights. But most of the plants had died. Childs knew this was not a growing light. Passing by the Cage, he counted four or five shelves cluttered with pots and trays full of dry earth and dead plants.

To the other side of the Cage sat the clothes bin. The

air was fouled by its smell. Childs stopped for a moment, watching clothes being dumped into a large wooden tub which began sloshing them around. In one tub the wash had finished and the men climbed down into it by narrow ladders. They threw the clothes (each piece marked with a prisoner's name) into baskets which were hauled up by hand-worked pulleys. Childs looked for Hawkins but did not see him.

Near the back of the building many of the men stuffed cotton into their ears because of the wringer—a huge machine which reached almost to the ceiling and which, in this mean light, could not be seen very well, though it could always be heard. Sounding to Childs like a great grinder and masher of bones—thundering, pounding. Row upon row of worn rollers squeezing out the water, which rushed down like a gray fall. Childs knew the men who worked here must always be damp, the water rotting out their shoes.

Montana was waiting for him at the stairway beside the wringer which led into the basement. Cutting his eyes across Childs, Red descended the stairs. Childs followed. Darkness. The smell of rotting wood. Montana stopped at a door, knocked four times.

"Yeah?"

"Red. Open up."

A boy was standing in the thin light eating a piece of cake.

"Snack time?" Red asked with irritation.

The boy wiped his mouth, shifted the cake to his other hand. "I was by myself. Didn't see no harm in it."

Inside the room, Childs could feel the wringer vibrating overhead.

176

"How many tricks today?" Red asked.

"Couple."

"How many?"

"Three."

The room smelled of damp stone. In one corner Childs could see a pile of rags in the gray light. Country music twanged out of a transistor radio.

Montana Red put his hands on his hips, craning his head toward the boy. "You stink, Harper."

"Huh?"

"When's the last time you bathed?"

Gulping down the last bite of cake, Harper crossed his arms, tucking his hands under his armpits.

Red turned to Childs. "You smell that, honey? Take a good nose full."

Childs's eyes and Harper's hit and at once broke away.

"Strip!" Montana said.

"I ain't got enough money for soap," Harper said.

"You make enough. Strip!"

Awkwardly, Harper began pulling off his clothes, trying to start a conversation. "Lot more guys been screwing. Like it was the end of the world or something. They say the silver count's low, too. What do you think?" he asked, naked, looking mildly at Childs.

Childs shook his head, felt embarrassed.

Hands behind his back, Montana slowly strolled around Harper twice. "Fifteen years I've been here and never seen anything so filthy. You know something?" Red grabbed Harper's face by the chin. "Look at me! Look straight at me! You know what you look like, smell like?"

"No."

"A nigger," Red said, flashing his teeth.

"I don't either."

"A nigger! Nigger! Nigger!" Red shouted, his finger stabbing Harper in the chest each time he said the word. "Now—you say it. You say 'I'm a nigger.'"

"Red—" Childs said.

"You shut up, lover. You shut up and get an eye full." Again Red turned to Harper. "Say it!"

"It ain't so."

"I think it is," Montana said in big whispers, inching closer, clasping Harper by the elbows. "And you better say it or you won't have a job. You won't have a cent for nothing. No clothes, no medicines, no smokes. . . ."

"Nigger," Harper murmured, dropping his face on his chest.

"That's not what I want. No, no. Tell me what you are. Tell this handsome young man here what you are."

Harper was shivering, moving his hands from his waist to his butt. "I'm a nigger," he said in a low voice.

Childs felt ashamed and cold.

A smile flickered across Montana's face. "There you go. Yes. Yes, you are a nigger. Now I'll tell you what. You go see Sergeant Greggs and tell him I sent you for some soap and powder. Will you do that?"

Harper nodded.

Drawing a handkerchief out of his pocket, Montana wiped his hands. "Danny," he said, looking at Childs softly, "don't be vain. Don't try to get away with more than you're worth." He paused at the door, then disappeared.

Just as Montana came up the stairwell, someone grabbed him by the neck, pushed him against the wall.

178

"Take it easy, Hawk," Montana said, trying to break the grip around his throat.

"Why?" Hawkins asked, ramming Red harder against the wall.

"Just ease up."

"The kid's got something wrong upstairs, Red. Why don't *you* ease up on Childs?" Hawkins jerked his hands away.

"He came to me," Montana said in a rasping voice. "Stuckey."

"Sure."

"The kid made the deal, not me."

"Stuckey ain't got a season ticket in this ball park either. He better watch his ass."

"You got something for this kid?" Red asked.

"I got something for you, Red. You can wear it in your belly and hang doughnuts on it."

"Thing about hawks is—sooner or later, they all get shot out of the big, blue sky."

"I know the kid owes you a few flinks. Okay, let him work them off. But after that, you let him down, got it?"

Red toyed with the rhinestone in his ear. "I service a lot of the Muslim's boys, awful lot. He gets—upset when his service is disturbed."

"Twenty, thirty guys here—they don't like to see this kind of thing happen to a kid. Makes them feel bad, and then, well, then they get mighty tough."

"The Muslim, Hawk. I just couldn't tell you how many men he's greased."

"Ain't you heard the tom-toms? Muslim's got a big monkey on his back. A big, black one, and he's coming down."

Red adjusted his collar and moved out of the stairwell.

"You let the kid down, Red," said Hawkins. "You put him on the ground or you go under it."

Montana Red dissolved into the darkness of the laundry.

"I just thought . . ." Childs began, but couldn't finish, moving backward towards the door.

Harper was turning up the radio. "One thing. You're nice looking. Better looking than me. But he won't keep you long. You make your money while you can. You do that here."

"Sure," Childs whispered, feeling the darkness of the stairwell envelop him. "Sure." But to himself he added that he would be free of Montana Red.

As Childs was pulling open his cell door, thinking about what Harper had said, he felt something dragging by the lower bars. At first he thought it was a dead rat, but stooping down, looking closer, he saw the limp puppy, a trace of blood running from its ear.

6

"WE hit the Muslim," he starts yelling at me. I don't know, three or four times this week he's been waking up at night screaming and hollering ever since he talked to Jones couple days ago. I had to start sleeping in his cell. Once, half asleep—get this now—woke me up about 3 A.M. and told me to go warn the Muslim that something was coming for them, going to get them both. Oh, I've seen these things before when we were in school. We'd be reading or in a lab or something, and all of a sudden it would hit him. Hell, I've seen him lock himself up in closets, climb under beds, shaking like a syph case. Even puke sometimes. Said it felt like everything was ending. Something was wrong and everything was falling to pieces inside himself—the universe, too. Oh yeah, planets and stars, everything going down to destruction

181

and there was nothing he could do about it. Three nights ago, when it got real bad, I gave him a Bible—his father used to read it to him when he was a kid—and he thumbed it for a while, then his face, eyes, got all dark and tight and he stared at me. Stared at me real funny. I known him a long time and, hell, I don't think I've ever seen him look like that. So now I just try to tell him everything's all right. Put my arms around him. Seems to help. That is, till last night. Same thing—shaking, all huddled up in the corner, and then just like that he says, "We hit the Muslim." Never blinked his eyes. Said we get him, like he didn't have a choice about it. Maybe he's right. Maybe it's the only thing we can do now. But he should have thought about it a little longer. You got to have a reason to kill a man. You at least got to have that.

So it's Darcy and me and Brown now. We're supposed to figure out the setup on the Muslim. God, how I hate that sonofabitch Darcy! There's something in him. At night—I swear to God—I've seen packs of cats following him around. Don't trust him either. Hell, right now he's probably working for the Muslim again. One day he'll turn. And if the Muslim finds out he's supposed to be hit—it's over. Simple as that. They'll get Moultrie and me if they have to saw through the bars. 'Course Moultrie sent word to the Muslim that he wanted to talk this thing out a week ago. Even set up a day for it. But I think it was just to catch him off guard. Yeah, I think Moultrie's had it in his mind to kill the Muslim since the first day he got here. Just been hiding from it. Maybe that's what brought on these spells again.

I just wish Moultrie hadn't brought in those guns.

There's a balance here, man. It's something everybody can feel. Bringing in hardware and knocking off the Muslim could bring this whole place down. I know that, but we started this stew and we're going to have to eat it. Another time things might have been easier. Everything got out of joint at once. The beekeeper, then Kate gets it, and Peterson—plink. Whores all upset, threatening each other about this Childs kid. I don't know, man—it just all went bad at once. All at once. Shit.

7

FATHER White placed a stepladder against the wall
and climbed three steps up. Tying one corner of the banner and then the other to the bars of the window, he
came down, looked at it: "Freedom Is Being Together."
The red and green showed up well against the cold
stone of the chapel. He rubbed a hand across his sore
belly, yawning. Last night he had stayed much too late.
He would have to watch that. Gently he touched a finger
to his still puffy black eye. He had grown used to wearing
it now like a badge. Proud of it even. Believing it gave
the inmates confidence in him. Showed them that he
wasn't afraid to stand up to Breen. Not that he did not
feel compassion for the old badger. But he had learned
that, behind all the weight lifting and loud talk, Breen
was afraid. Afraid that he had spent almost ten years of
his life here and hadn't done a thing for the men. Well,

there was some new blood in the prison now and things would be different.

White was dragging the ladder to the rear of the chapel when Breen stepped out onto the altar. Coming up from genuflection, Breen laid a handful of flowers before the tabernacle. Roughly he stuffed them into two vases, trying to make some sort of arrangement. He kneeled for a moment, then turned.

White saw Breen's face catch the banner, grimace, then scowl—typical of the tough, old church, Irish sentiment that was so ridiculous.

"Rice Jarvis, you know him?" Breen asked.

"Big guy? Got a moustache?"

"Short. Clean shaven. He's in your—experiment."

"There are about forty guys in this program. Their faces I don't remember."

"You put him with Shelty. Jarvis *was* an AA guy. Now after eight years he's drinking again. Two drunks in one cell."

"It'll change."

Breen scraped a hand across his rough chin, then shoveled both of his hands under his cincture. "Eight years. Eight years Jarvis let the stuff alone. You know how he's feeling now?"

"When you left Rome you beat the booze alone in the jungle. Everybody knows that."

"Shut up about that and listen. It's like your head's a can of worms. Squirming around, screwing out your ears. It's like you want to open your head and scoop out the maggots."

"Everyone isn't a tough guy. Together they'll beat it. Shelty and the other one."

"Who?"

"The guy you're so steamed up about."

"You don't even remember his name now, do you?"

"Names don't interest me, Father. It's suffering. I want to end it." White said, watching Breen's hands and keeping his own above his waist.

Breen slammed his hands on a pew, leaning forward. "You dumb sonofabitch," he said, flicking his eyes towards the altar. "Names and faces you don't remember? You tell me what else these guys have got here?"

"Look, it's one lousy guy. Out of forty men getting help, recovering, one lousy . . ."

"Drunk?"

"Yeah, that's right. One stinking drunk. I've lived with it. I've been on the other end. I saw what my father did to all of us. And I learned, see? I found out how to handle it. You hit them hard. You make the bastards look at what they are. You beat their heads with it again and again and again until they see what they must do."

Craning his head toward the ceiling, searching it, Breen blew out a hard breath. "You're ruining a good man, White. He's got a family, too. And they won't know that poor, slobbering sack of guts come visiting day."

"Forty other men. They're doing alright."

"You sure?"

"Ask them."

"Odds that in sixty percent of your 'experimental cells' there's shaving lotion, extract, or maybe just pure corn."

"The program's working."

Breen was clenching his fists at his chest. "Souls, Father. Did they teach you about souls in the seminary?"

186

"I'm not stopping this aid because one slob hasn't got the guts to put the bottle away!"

Breen watched White walking down the aisle toward the rectory. "You're right, Father. You're right. You shouldn't stop this thing because one—slob—hasn't got the guts to put the bottle away. You should stop it because one good man took the bottle out again."

White paused at the door, then eased out, never looking back.

All during the day, the problem boiled bitterly in Breen. Jarvis would not be the only man to fall.

At nine thirty Breen went down to the leather shop. Opened the door into the rich, slow scent of glues and dyes, dark and thick; of harnesses and stirrups. Through the shop's north wall, almost entirely paned with glass, were blinking the late October stars. Cowboy was sitting in his wheelchair, etching something into the south wall. Breen propped himself against the door, watching quietly. The south wall ran forty feet long and nine feet high and from ceiling to floor was sheeted in squares of leather. For almost six years Cowboy had been working on the mural and about one-third of the leather was filled with buffalo clustered and tiny in the vast, sandy distance. In the foreground an angry bull glared from a swirl of dust, one foot raised in fury, the thick shoulders snared in a tangle of matted hair. Behind the bull rose sharp swells of tortured mountains, while beneath them were blowing barrages of sagebrush, whirlwinds of sand. Just at the protruding light switch Breen could see the mischievous eyes of a prairie dog peeping from its hole, and near the mural's center, hand slanted over his eyes,

187

amulets and bones dangling from his lean neck, a Sioux warrior was scouting the distance.

Breen approached Cowboy quietly from behind. A little man. A thin, rough body. The face slouching low and worn between his slick forehead and horn chin. The old, greasy hat; the red, starred boots.

"Toad's not bad," Breen said loudly, hoping for a start.

"Toad's the hardest thing," said Cowboy, without a flinch turning to Breen.

Breen examined the horned toad carefully.

"A little fat, maybe?" Cowboy asked, setting down the electric burning-tool on the floor.

"Could be," Breen said, running his fingers over the new work.

"Now your Indian up here . . ." Cowboy tossed his head toward the warrior. "Da Vinci."

Breen cocked his head. "You got the good lines."

"The cavalry you can cover up with uniforms. On Indians, you got to see skin and bone. Spent three months copying Da Vinci. Working on that buck."

Breen dragged up a stool, was staking his feet in the braces. "You're good at this. You should be outside."

"Hell, that's no way to live."

"You could teach. You could have sidewalk shows."

A dry, red tongue flicked in and out of Cowboy's mouth. "You know what you got to have out there?"

"Whiskey and women?"

"Bed and bread, and I got it right here."

Breen smiled, slapped his hands together. "I've come to talk about White."

Cowboy pushed up his hat with a thick thumb. "Don't like him too good, do you?"

"We get along," Breen said.

"Must have been that left hook that did all the damage."

"You heard about that?"

"No, I made it up."

Breen scratched at his jaw. "Alright, he's a punk and I don't care who knows what I think. But this plan of his—it's screwing up some good men."

"Jarvis?"

"Eight years, Cowboy."

"More or less."

"You know this idea's no good for you, either."

Cowboy licked his thumb, swabbed the tips of his boots. "He's got me and crazy ole Waldrop celling together now." He glanced at Breen, eyes hard as shoe peg corn. "Ain't touched the sauce in two weeks."

"I tell you it's a crummy plan."

"In the night, I used to wake up. I used to get scared, lonesome. I used to belt it down real good in the night."

"Jarvis won't be the only one."

"What's the matter? You afraid they're putting you out to pasture?"

"Where's the bottle?" Breen said, standing up, hauling up his trousers.

"I tell you it's been two weeks."

Breen began hunting through nearby piles of scrapped leather, rags, cans. In a few minutes he stopped, taking a deep breath, glaring at Cowboy's boots. "Take them off."

"Kid's like sand in your eyes, ain't he?"

Lifting up one of Cowboy's legs, Breen tugged off a boot, looked inside—empty.

"Why don't you take a gander at the other one?"

189

When Breen pulled out the thin, warm bottle of lemon extract, Cowboy was grinning.

"Framed."

"Horseshit!"

"Honest to God. Two weeks. The bottle's full."

Breen checked it against the light.

"At night, when the fever starts rising in your throat, it helps to have somebody around who's felt the same thing."

"Look at me, Cowboy." Breen took a firm hold of the sharp, flinty chin, and turned his face toward him. "Look at this mug. It's sucked dry more bottles than you've seen. Nothing helps. You know that. Not until *you* decide to beat it. And I don't want any suicides by drunks after visiting day. You've seen it and so have I. Now you get these guys together and you tell them I said to dump this program. Got it?"

"Sure," Cowboy said, turning his face down, staring at his boots.

"And if you need to talk to someone at night—it's me, buddy. The way it's always been!"

As Breen scuffed back down the stale Tunnel, pushing away all questions of motive, he noticed the security door of the rectory open slowly. Quickly he ducked into the doorway of the post office. From the rectory, dressed in jeans and a T-shirt, Father White emerged, carefully looking around, then moving down the Tunnel. Breen pressed himself into the dark of the doorway. White passed, approached Building Three. A boy darted out of the shadows. They moved close to one another saying something and White gently swatted him on the butt as they slipped into the dark entrance of Building Three.

190

Breen pressed his forehead against the wall. The sewing and the pretty hands and the crazy ideas. It should have told him the story. *A fag! Holy God!* He swept a hand through his hair and started toward the building entrance. There was nothing to do but end it. At the top of the stairs he glanced toward the gate—locked, a guard rocking on his heels behind the bars. Another door, the one leading to the old gym was part way open. He could hear counting, though muffled and low.

Peeping through the door—fifteen or twenty men, barefoot, a few in red jerseys, doing calisthenics, and White standing before a blackboard full of football plays.

A great rush of anger and relief as he picked his way back to the Tunnel. But Breen felt, too, the smallest bit of respect for White. *He's dead wrong about Cowboy, Jarvis, and the others. But he's tough. That's something. He's tough and gutty.*

8

CHILDS had just finished a bad argument with Red. He had been with him almost four weeks, and every day Montana's jealousy grew. Trying to settle himself down, thinking of what to do, he paced slowly around Building One, finally ending up on the fourth tier staring down at E-Block—a group of cells that rose in the center of the building as high as the third tier. Prisoners were confined to these cells for minor offenses: back talking a guard, not taking off a hat in the cafeteria.

Childs could see above each cell one glaring light which apparently was never shut off. Because of nearby steam pipes, the men sweated continually, stripped down to undershorts. A drain in the left corner of the cell served as a commode. Childs had heard that if a man became rowdy, the drain was blocked. There were no mattresses, sheets, or pillows. The floor of the cells were filled with shredded newspapers which absorbed moisture and where roaches and mice scrambled for crumbs. Childs had been told that often men awoke to find their fingernails chewed by rats in the night and that some men crammed tissue into their ears to keep out the roaches. Glad to be away from Montana, he listened to those in lockup calling out their letters or messages to friends on the third tier who were taking them down.

"Say . . . well, just say . . . Daddy loves you and don't forget to come and see Daddy on Christmas 'cause you know he misses you very, very much. You got that? And say that Daddy's made a surprise and he'll have it ready for Christmas Day and it's . . . beads and leather and . . . say it's a surprise."
and

"You tell that sonofabitch, Jack—I said you tell that miserable bastard to get me out of this stinking hole. I've had it up to here, and I'm not trash, you know."
and

"She's got enough goddamned money as it is. All I want is enough for smokes, for God's sake."
and

"Will you please tell Jenny—now, you got to make this plain—tell Jenny that she has to get oil now before the cold sets in or she'll get caught in the rush."
and

"I can't hear you."

"Onions, goddammit! I don't want any goddamned onions on my chili."
and

"Is he alright now is what I'm asking. Will he make it?"

"Yeah. She says his ticker's good, too."

"What?"

"His heart. The doctor says it's holding up."
and
"What the hell are you doing, Mike?"

"Throwing a kiss."

"You're what?"

"She said to throw you a smacker."

"Oh, for Christ's sake, Mike."

Then, "Childs!" someone called from below on the first floor. "Daniel Childs!"

"Yeah?"

"You got visitors."

He could see them through the bars of the last gate. His father nervously flicking his cigarette, his face lean and tense. His mother rubbing her big hands together. And as Childs moved toward them, his father's face rose like something out of his own heart, strong and good and tender, while his mother gazed at him, brittle and strict. They hugged one another for a moment, then his mother cleared her throat, broke them up as she sat down.

"You look good, son. My God! You even put on a little weight."

"Even got a little pot now," his father said, rolling his hand across his son's stomach. He caught Childs staring at his blue-stained hands. "Oh, they made me a dyer. Out of that goddamned carding room for good now. Look here what I brung you." His hands scrambled through his coat pocket. Pulled out two large match boxes. "Didn't know if they'd let me bring them in."

Raisins, Childs knew. The sweet, rich smell. "I ain't had any in a long time," he said.

"What's that you got in your ear, son?" his mother asked.

194

Childs felt his hand shoot up for his ear. Stunned that he had forgotten the rhinestone.

"Looks like an ear bob," she said, squinting.

"Mr. Connor, he's been missing you at the mill. Says he just can't find starch like you no more," his father said.

"Son? You taken to wearing ear bobs?"

Childs could smell the brown, homemade beer, as his father's body slid closer to him.

"Now don't you pay no attention to your mama. She's just all het up 'cause we had that flat."

"I won it. It's—a poker prize, Mama."

Mary Childs felt hurt somewhere. She saw a difference in her son's eyes, smelling a sweetness from him. "What are you wearing, son? What's that smell?"

"Shaving lotion," his father said. "Our boy's done took to shaving, Mama. Ain't that something?"

Childs began unraveling in his chest, couldn't meet his mother's eyes. "I'm not awful good with the razor yet." His mother's woody hand slid across his face.

"Peach fuzz. No cutting there. What is it you're wearing? What happened?"

"You hush. You just hush, Mary. It's a little toilet water, that's all."

Mary Childs looked carefully over her son. New pants, new shoes. The eyes weren't his anymore. "What you done to your eyes, son? Look here. What have you done to yourself?"

She put a hand on his neck. Her skin felt rough and moist as if with hen's blood. And he felt his face now light up and flare like kindling. "Mama, I—I done something."

Her face turned hard. Eyes and mouth losing light.

"Danny, start your prayer language. Let me hear it."

"Hush, hush," his father said, laying one arm around him.

"Suppertime, Mama. They make us eat early. I got to go." He tried to pry away from his father.

"Take that out," she said, pointing at his ear.

"Won't do no good," Childs said, gently breaking his father's grip.

Mary Childs rose from the chair, face sharp, ashes, fallen deeply. "Take that thing out!"

Pulling his father's arm away, he pushed the blue hand against the table and saw a mask rise to the surface of his father's face. He stood up, feeling part of himself sift away like smoke. "It's me, Mama. It's—me."

"No," his mother said. Then yelled, "No! No! No!" Grabbing him by the throat, she pulled quickly at the rhinestone. Blood and pain and the stone in his mother's bloody palm.

"You see there? You see it? Now, come here!"

She dragged him to the water cooler and tore open his shirt.

"Now, you wash. You wash yourself clean of this filthiness."

Childs felt the big hands ramming his head beneath the stream of freezing water. The handkerchief scrubbing his face and neck.

A guard rushed in, pulled Mary Childs back. "What the hell's wrong with you, lady?"

"Look at him," his mother yelled, then dropped her voice, her face. "Look what you done to my boy. A queer! You made him a goddamned queer. Oh, my God. Oh, Jesus."

196

Somehow he made it back to Building One and found himself standing before Rose's cell, holding his hand to his ear, feeling hurt and lost. Remembering, as if by some new instinct, that many boys had come to Rose for help. To Rose, who had lived here so long and been loved by so many. To Rose, who was rocking in her cane chair, taking down her shoulder-length white braids. Ferns lined the walls and the cell smelled earthy and green.

"If you have finished looking, go away. If you wish to speak, then come in."

Once inside, the air smelled of ferns and mints and rouge. The cold sun silhouetted the figure Childs had never seen before.

Rose brushed out her long white hair. Her face was mottled, knit tightly together like a shawl. A long scar ran down her neck and vanished into her clothing. "Yellow hair and blue eyes—you have aroused a great many hearts." She pointed at a crystal candy dish. "A lemon drop."

As Childs reached for the candy, he felt a hand grab his butt, pinch him hard. It shook him, but he turned to hand her the dish.

She popped the candy into her mouth. "Feels good and solid. If those go soft, you will lose many hearts. It takes strength to hold them here."

"I heard a lot about you. I come to ask a question."

"Now, when I speak to you, do not look at your watch or scratch your ear or shuffle your feet. Just quietly sit down."

As Childs was squatting down, he noticed on a shelf above her head a bell jar of hummingbirds which seemed

197

lifelike, four or five china plates, and as many crystal glasses.

"You think you are in love."

"No," Childs said.

Rose pursed her lips. Her sly eyes searched the boy before her, catching the dried blood on his ear, between his fingers. "Ah," she said softly. "No worth. Despicable. You have come to these opinions?"

In some way Childs felt comforted by Rose's strange manner of speaking. "My folks came to see me today."

"And you rejoiced?"

"We hugged up a little bit."

"And after that?"

"My mama saw the ear bob. I'd left it in. My mama, she saw the ear bob and yanked it out."

"You felt pity for her."

"She didn't understand me, what happened to me."

"But you understood her and what she saw?"

"No."

"I will have a peppermint now."

Childs handed her another dish, careful this time not to turn his back.

Clicking the peppermint around in her mouth, Rose rested her face on both hands, elbows propped on the chair arms. "She saw what had been her own flesh sitting corrupted before her."

"Wasn't no choice."

"Not for her and not for you. Here you cannot choose. Outside you dare not."

"I don't know what to do. I lost them, my folks. I lost them for good. And Montana, I don't get along with him at all no more."

"Montana Red is displeased with you?"

"He ain't nothing but a whore."

"So are you a whore."

Childs blew out a puff of air, began to touch his ear.

"Put your hand away and look at me."

Tucking his hand into his pocket, Childs looked up at the sagging face, quick eyes.

Rose pointed at her heart. "Here lies the deepest thicket, and you must come to know it. Where to walk and where not to walk. Where to cut down and where to leave stand. Love your own goodness and be careful of what bad there is in you. Evil feeds upon goodness, but so does goodness temper itself with evil."

Childs closed his eyes a moment, trying to understand what Rose had said.

"Montana Red is unhappy with you because he has allowed himself to love you." Rose touched the scar on her neck. "This is the trail of a knife. It goes farther than you see. It got there because I loved once. Here, those who love murder or are murdered."

Turning in her chair, she took a half-opened rosebud from a small vase beside her bunk and handed it to Childs. "Yellow hair, *you* are the dancer now. Much will be offered and much more should be taken. Have your affairs, but when you have finished—hang their hearts outside your door like corn shucks. And when you lie in bed alone, belong only to yourself."

A wave of her hand told Childs he had been dismissed. Holding the rose carefully, he moved out into the darkness of the tiers.

I T was five fifteen and Warden Jesse Cates still paced the gunboards of tower two some forty minutes after the football game. He knew the prison was off center and tight, but he had hoped that the game would let off some pressure. It had been a bad choice. Tower two directly overlooked the playing field and the team benches, and Cates kept thinking that he should have stopped the game early.

The Blue team hustled out calisthenics while Breen yelled last-minute instructions.

Looking nervously away from their competition, the Red team strained to hear White's plan.

Then the captains shook. A coin flashed. The lines formed. Knuckles into the grass. And Blue made the classic drive up the center, knocking Red ten yards back.

"Yeah! Yeah!" Breen shouted.

The teams set up again, and once more Blue rolled over the Red defense.

Breen jumped to his feet, thrashing his hands in the air.

White studied a chart. Sent in a new man.

Another play and Blue had the touchdown.

Cates watched the crowd. Almost a thousand prisoners on the bleachers. So far they seemed alright. He had twelve men in the towers. Six extra armed and waiting in the Gateroom. If Breen kept his head, there would be no trouble.

All the way to half time Blue hit hard and smart, though Red managed to hold them to fourteen points.

Around the Blue bench, the players drummed their helmets, slapped butts and hands. Shouted a few insults at their opponents.

Cates called up Breen on the tower phone.

"Keep them cool, Father."

"Look, Warden. It'll be alright."

"Your boys are getting a little too riled."

"Second half, they settle down."

"I'll watch it close. Trouble—and it's over."

"Got you," Breen said.

The Red bench seemed too quiet. The men huddled about White, who was talking with a fresh running back—P. G. Carter, his jersey read.

Cates remembered him. An all-state running back turned burglar and junkie. Too bad.

In the first part of half time, the crowd seemed uneasy. Then the Broad River Prison Band hauled their equipment onto the field and began picking out mountain music: the metal ping of the flat-picked guitar slatting against the banjo and the shuttlings of the mandolin and sawings of the fiddle. Good tunes born in the glens of the moonshine mountains.

The players bucked back into their gear. Milled around the sidelines. P. G. Carter loped out toward the field. The Red looked enthusiastic about him. But in the first few plays Carter did them no good. Red lost thirty yards, just barely holding Blue at the goal. Still fourteen to nothing. Then on a run back, Carter suddenly broke free, found his feet. He faked right, swerved left, wove in and out, and scored.

Most of the prisoners roared and cheered. Whores threw handkerchiefs. Shop men slugged one another on the back.

"Calm down! Take it easy. Just somebody wipe that junkie out next time!" Breen yelled.

Cates got on the phone, ordered up the men in the Gateroom. Told them not to load their weapons.

Blue had the ball, fumbled it. Red took over on Blue's forty. Again Carter down the lane, getting the good blocks. Touchdown.

Part of the bleachers emptied out onto the field. The four field officers tried to push them back.

Cates advised the guntowers to open windows, go to port arms. Got Breen on the horn.

"Yeah?"

"Breen, you get your players off that field!"

"Can't hear you, Warden," Breen yelled.

Cates quickly climbed down from the tower. Got his extra men behind him. "Load your weapons." He arrived at the field gate just in time to see Breen pitch his quarterback out of the game and jam on a helmet.

"Cream their ass!" he yelled to the team.

"They're hitting like hell, coach."

"Piss on them."

Breen called out signals while White was yelling protests.

Cates positioned his men in the killing zone. Waiting.

Looking to pass, Breen faked, then barreled straight into the Red line. Took a blow to the head. Kept going. Clothes lined. Drove ahead. Broke two tackles and looked like he had the score, then suddenly a red jersey flew off the sidelines and slammed hard into his knees and blew him down—P. G. Carter!

The benches and bleachers completely emptied. Thirty or forty men began swinging.

Cates called for three volleys from the killing zone. The tower guards drew their beads. Another volley from the killing zone, and the prisoners turned to look at the towers. Taking in the guns. The smoking barrels in the killing zone.

Most of the fighting stopped. The field officers began moving prisoners toward the ramps that led back into the cell blocks.

From tower two, Jesse Cates looked again across the empty field and then turned to gaze at the prison. Going through with the game had been damn stupid. He had had a choice about that and blown it. But there were some things he could not affect. Freeman's hurt pride. The murders of molesters and whores. Nigger power struggles. Even so, these occurrences were business as usual, survivable—*if* they were staggered, came one at a time. Somehow that had not happened this time. Somehow he was getting screwed all at once, by everything, and it made him angry. But there was nothing to do but watch. Watch and move quick when it all finally went up like a hand grenade in a can of shit.

10

Two days after the football game, in the evening, Spoons was watching nervously in Moultrie's cell. "When do you think it will happen?"

"Look at her eyes. See how the pupils open and close?"

"The storm probably scares her," Spoons said.

"Her breathing's faster now."

"He'll kill them, the tom. You know that?"

"We'll have to seal up the door somehow. Wire maybe," Moultrie said, feeling a spray of rain against his face from the open cell window.

"Lots of blood, I guess."

"Sacks."

"Huh?"

"They come real neat and clean in sacks. No blood. You wait and see."

Outside, a storm made distant rumbling, flashes of light.

On his bunk, the Muslim is doing sit-ups. Wearing headphones and listening to the *Pastoral Symphony* on his stereo. Lying back, breathing hard, he grabs hold of his belly and shakes it. Down below he hears the night vendors calling out: "Popcorn, sandwiches, drinks—before you catch your winks. Popcorn, sandwiches . . ."

The scales tell him he's lost a little weight. Puts on his dark purple robe. Sprays himself with lime perfume. Hitches his shoulders and shivers because of the dampness brought on by the storm.

The cat lay quietly on her side, twitching her tail, her belly swollen and tight.

"Put your hands there," Moultrie said.

"Where?"

"Give me. Right there. Feel them?"

Quickly Spoons withdrew his hand. "Gives me the creeps."

"Wait a minute," Moultrie said, hearing a cry out in the darkness.

"What?"

"You hear that? It's the tom. He's out there."

"I heard him."

"Smells the birthing probably. Wants to kill her for it."

"Maybe we should close the window." Spoons was rising, his brace rattling.

"No. Leave it open. I like the rain."

Scuffing leather down toward the showers. The Muslim resolving to buy a new pair of sandals, these too noisy.

205

Smelling now roach poison, coffee, the water drumming in the showers, not the fresh water from the storm. Hears something behind him—a cat, crying wild and ragged in the dark.

"Hungry. Ought to be fed," he says to one of the two shadows that follow him everywhere, even to his shower.

Hesitating at the shower entrance. One overhead light is out. Not recognizing two forms in the dimness and steam, searching for their faces. "Is one light enough, brothers?" he says, carefully watching.

"It's all we need."

The voice is not familiar, but neither does it sound dangerous. Rain lashes through the open window. "Well, brothers, half light is better than none, is it not?"

Posts his men at the entrance. Feels safer under the warm water, but does not turn his back to those he cannot see. And from somewhere in the showers, something familiar arises, an odor, but as quickly disappears. Hides itself beneath the steam. The Muslim lathers his washcloth with his own scented soap.

The cat's belly began heaving.

"What do we do? My God!"

"Watch her. Watch the beauty of it," Moultrie said, again feeling the tight belly.

"It's awful. I hate it."

Slowly the first kitten began to emerge, glistening dark through the tissue, mouth and feet struggling in the new air.

*   *   *

It began as a feeling, then a vibration, and then a final and dark recognition of what was hiding so well behind the stale smell of steam—Darcy!

Turning toward the door, wishing to cry out to his men, but thinking better of it, continuing to wash, rub himself with the cloth. Then thinking quickly—yes, yes! A ruse. Pretend to drop the soap. And as he bends down, blood thundering in his ears, gathers himself and springs for the door.

The first blow came in low, just beneath the center of his spine and shook him hard, though no pain, no pain— and he would have cried out, made it to the door, but for the arm around his neck, the wet, thin body that pulled him backward. And it was the second blade across his abdomen that brought the sudden loss of weight, weakness, the unfamiliar lights. And on the floor groping toward the entrance, he felt a cold sheet of rain, then darkness . . . deafness . . . less . . . nothing.

"Shut that window," Moultrie said.

The cat was cleaning her new brood.

"What time is it?"

Spoons looked at his watch. "Nine thirty."

"He should be showering just about now."

THREE

STANDING in the cafeteria the morning after the Muslim's death, Langford Cays could feel an energy and strain in the air. In the past few months he knew the prisoners had stowed away too many threats and uncertainties into themselves, too many deaths and omens. He knew too that he should not be in the cafeteria. That it was a fire watch or something worse. But where could he go?

He was moving to break up a few guards who had collected near one of the building's doors when something sailed from a gang of Muslims and struck a couple of Moultrie's men. Suddenly the two groups rushed each other. Both feeding lines broke apart then, began to throw trays and silver, overturn tables. The guards who had been standing at the doors disappeared up the Tunnel. White men plugged the entrances, scrambling to get out. Cays knew better than to try now. His best bet was the kitchens or windows. Quickly he tossed off his hat, climbed beneath a line of milk machines. By then the prisoners were tearing down signs and doors; driving spoons and forks into the stone walls.

He had to get some kind of weapon—a good piece of wood, chair leg, but he made himself wait; hoping they would desert the building soon. A few men pounded salt shakers against pine cabinets until the glass burst in their hands and, catching the shards, some nearly severed off whole fingers grinding pieces of glass into wooden tables, the tile floor. On the left-hand side of the building scores of men attacked blank stone with table legs and spoons. And when the first block was pried loose, they gave a shrill shout and ripped down half of the north wall, revealing the quiet Yard.

Cays saw his chance now. Stripping off his uniform shirt and tie, he crawled from beneath the machines, looked toward the doors to the Tunnel—still blocked. The north wall streamed with men—no good. The kitchens were his only chance. Grabbing up a window bar, he dodged into a small pack of men, keeping his face low, and joined in ramming a kitchen door. In a few seconds the casement gave way and the door rumbled down. Dancing in the fallen stone and chunks of plaster, the prisoners rubbed powder and dust into their faces and hair, then charged the kitchen.

Cays smeared his face with dust as well. Anything to hide. Inside, two mess officers lay unconscious beneath a window which they had partially broken through. Huge pots of vegetables were boiling over, hissing into the gas

212

burners beneath them. From one small ramp near the ceiling, two prisoners shoved an officer into a vat of bubbling tomatoes. While he screamed the prisoners zipped open their flies and began pissing on him.

Climbing onto a table, Cays leapt toward the smashed window. He tried to squeeze through the remaining bars, but could not. With a loose brick he hammered the other bars, holding himself above the floor with one hand. Just as one bar broke free, he felt someone grab his leg. He looked down to see a wild black face screaming: "It's a screw! A honky screw!" Several other niggers rushed toward him. Cays kicked the nigger holding him in the forehead, felt a soft crunch as the man fell away. With the last of his strength, he jammed himself through the window and fell onto the pavement of the Yard.

For a moment he lay dazed, then felt his thigh spread with a sticky warmth. Blood was running down his left arm from a long gash. Feeling dizzy and sick, he looked toward the guntowers, but figured he might be shot down in the confusion. The front gate was the only way out and somehow he had to get into the Tunnel. The Yard door was clogged with men, so keeping a tight grip on his left arm he made his way across the blacktop to the infirmary. Most of the glass and bars had been broken out. Hurriedly checking for any glass, he dived into a window and slipped down into the infirmary. The air smelled better. Small fires were burning, several prisoners stoking the flames with sheets, paper, specimens of blood and urine. Others downed bottles of pills and liquids, stuck needles into their veins. Cays found a rag and quickly made a tourniquet for his arm. But lights whirled before his eyes now and as he staggered by the dentist's

213

office he thought he saw him strapped in his own chair, screaming, while one prisoner held his mouth open and another approached him with the whirring drill. Finally he made it through the unlocked security door and out into the Tunnel. Weaving up the Tunnel toward the front gate amidst hundreds of men, he could hear a thundering and grinding from those cell blocks still locked up, a huge single voice chanting: "Kill! Kill! Kill!"

Near the first set of stairs, he was knocked down, but did not allow himself to go out. He began crawling. Made it to the top and within sight of Carter's gate. He couldn't feel his arm anymore. No focus to his eyes, everything was gray and fading. Then twenty feet from Carter's gate he saw a face, a hand reaching out between the bars—Walsh. Cays on his belly now, wiggling towards the bars. But it didn't matter, he was safe now, safe. He lifted his hand toward Walsh, then shuddered from a heavy jolt, thunder at the back of his head. Going down he heard his teeth crack as his face hit the concrete floor, going down to blackness.

When the cafeteria blew, Hawkins knew the shops and laundry would go up next. There was one safe place for him—his cell. He and most of the other white men began to slip out of the building. The niggers stayed and went crazy. It was their ball game and they would play. In the maintenance bins near the wringer, they were dumping buckets of paint all over each other, turning red and green, yellow and white. With blue-flamed torches they cut through steel doors, chased retreating guards, and fought one another. Just outside the Cage three of them had pinned a white boy to the floor. They were stripping off his clothes, one already spreading the boy's legs. "Bastards," Hawkins mumbled, looking for something. He picked up a two-by-four, crept up behind them, and slugged the one kneeling to do his business square across the neck. When another spun around with a shiv, Hawkins rammed the board into his belly, then neatly clipped him on the chin. The third man made a motion for his pocket and Hawkins took a good grip on the two-by-four, patted it against the side of his hand and, grinning, motioned him forward: "Come here, pickaninny. We going to play a little ball, me and you." The nigger glanced around, then took off toward the door. The white boy motioned he was alright and Hawkins raced to the laundry gate. Just above him, high on a ladder, an old man unscrewed the outer covering of a shift bell, stuffed cotton easily against the drum, then screwed the covering back into place and carefully began climbing down.

"Shit!" Hawkins said when he got out onto the black-top. Half the prison seemed on fire. Niggers were flooding toward him from the Yard door and the caved-in wall of the cafeteria. From the back of the kitchens he saw a guard without his shirt. Bleeding badly, the guard ran toward the infirmary. Hawkins thought it was Cays, but lost sight of him in the crowd. For a moment, he thought about just whipping ass back to his cell, but the Yard was almost completely full now. It was no use. By the Industry Building he saw a silent group of white men. They were trapped too. Hawkins looked up at the gun-towers where the guards stood screaming into their phones, then back at the niggers. He dropped the board and walked toward the white men.

Most of the niggers became quiet now, staring back

at the prison, the blasted buildings and fires. The last one out was an old man. He shuffled into the Yard wearing pajamas, trailing what seemed to be a catheter tube from his fly. In his right hand he clenched a pillowcase, grease streaming down his arm. He poked his head into the pillow case and bobbed up with a mouthful of steaming meat. Turning toward the Tunnel, he flogged the bloody tube, filling the Yard with a gurgling laugh and the cracking catheter.

One of the others abruptly threw his booty toward the Tunnel and screamed, "Yea! Freedom!" Then the rest began throwing into the air whatever they had carried out with them. Hawkins watched a few niggers peel down their trousers. They painted bull's-eyes on each other's butts and wagged them at the tower guards. "Freedom! Freedom! Freedom!" they were shouting.

"Yeah," Hawkins said, looking up at the guntowers. "It's coming for you, you dumb bastards. Shit!" He spit and moved deeper into the white men. Waiting.

Moultrie had moved to the Yard and made his plans quickly.

"I knew this thing was coming. All along I could feel it," Spoons said.

"You're a liar," Moultrie said, scanning the Yard. The sun clattered about his eyes. The wind peddled scents of fire, of uncertain men and wasted food. . . . *But why shouldn't it work?*

"You shouldn't stay here."

"Hell."

"The Muslim had a lot of friends."

"Then this will separate the niggers from the brothers.

216

Is Jones out here? Get him, some of his boys. We need barricades, food depots."

"Do you know what you're saying?"

"Round up all the screws and honkies. Put ten men with shivs on them."

Moultrie pulled a plastic bag holding the two revolvers from his sweater. "Can Brown handle one of these things?"

Spoons slapped his brace, folded his arms. "Too many people against you, Moultrie. Screws, the Muslim's men."

"You pass the word. You let them know I've got some whammie here."

Spoons limped away muttering.

Moultrie was surveying the Yard. The roofs of the buildings. If they came, it would be straight out of the Tunnel. If they didn't come in the next half hour, it would be alright. Shoving the guns under his sweater, he quickly moved into the center of the Yard.

Warden Cates had called Breen and Freeman to his office. The light was dim and smoky.

"How many out there you figure?" Breen asked.

"Three, four hundred," the Warden said. "Tower men say it looks like they got seven guards, couple dozen white men."

"If you moved now, you could bust it up with sticks."

"No," Freeman said, hooking a thick finger around his cigar.

"Look, Freeman—you don't run in there blasting away like hell," Breen said.

"You want to match sticks against thirty-eights?" Freeman asked.

217

"What are you talking about?" Breen looked at the Warden. "They got guns?"

Jesse Cates sat down on his desk, sipping coffee. "Maybe."

"They got them," Freeman said, quietly sizing up Cates.

"What do you think, Freeman?" the Warden asked.

"Fifteen men. Shotguns. Twenty rounds apiece."

"I don't want another Attica."

"They waited at Attica. They talked a lot," Freeman said, screwing his cigar against an ashtray.

"You sure about the guns?" Breen asked quickly.

"Big as day, they're there," Freeman said.

The Warden had opened the curtains. The gray day was filling the room. "How many volleys?"

"Two, three probably."

"Can you promise that?"

"Depends on the guns. We knock out the artillery— no problem."

"The stupid bastards," Breen said, pulling at his collar. "The dumb sonofabitches!"

"Five rounds apiece," the Warden said.

"Ten."

"Goddamit, Freeman! I'm running this prison."

"If we hit them hard now, right now, it's over in ten minutes. If we don't fool around."

The Warden looked at Breen. A light rain began spattering the windows.

They were to go in now. Inside the Arsenal, slugging the shotguns full. The clacking, working sound of good metal. Walsh held the shotgun to his side with both hands and let his finger relax on the trigger guard. Listened to the other men swearing oaths to one another about what they would do. Remembered Cays being dragged back down into the prison, out of reach. A hostage.

"No man knocks off safety until I say," Freeman said, gripping his weapon. "No one takes his muzzle out of the sky until I say. On one, you lower the barrel. Two, you knock off the safety. Three—you pick your target and hold. If there's more, I'll give the order."

Silence.

"They got weapons?" someone asked.

"Could be," Freeman said.

"Watch your ass out there," Rhiner said, turning to Walsh.

"They got Cays."

"Yeah. Yeah, they do."

Walsh followed Rhiner and the others out into the Tunnel.

Childs had felt it in the cafeteria. Like a big snake coiled up in the corner. Cold and sick, licking everyone's eyes with its black tongue until they went crazy. He had hidden beneath a table during the viloence but somehow was swept out into the Yard, then corralled with the other white men in a corner between the Industry Building and the garbage bins. He wanted to stay close to John Hawkins.

Making tents out of blankets. Speaking quietly, directly to his men, Moultrie felt renewed. As if the dead parts of himself spit out the earth, rose from roots and darkness.

"Get the wounded brothers in here."

His men began bringing those injured during the rampage into the tents, out of the rain. Others were shoving desks, pieces of furniture out of the Industry Building for the barricade. But the Muslims sat in the center of their loot and refused to move, glaring at the revolver in Moultrie's belt.

Moultrie shivered in the rain. "Spoons," he said, fixing his gaze on the Muslims, "any spigots around here?"

"Couple."

"They'll cut off the water soon. Store as much as you can."

The Muslims' heads beaded with rain. Moultrie approached them. "Off your asses, brothers."

"Who says?"

Moultrie laid a thumb against the .38's rough hammer. "Right here."

Two men sneered and spat. Reaching into their socks, they flicked out long knives.

Brown loped up beside Moultrie, with a soft grin on his face, holding a pistol against his thigh.

The Muslims stood up in groups of two or three. More knives were drawn. "There ain't enough bullets in the whole world," one of them said.

"There's enough for you," Moultrie said.

The Tunnel door slammed loudly against the wall as the guards quickly filed out into the Yard, shotguns ready. Most of the Muslims quickly fell back. A few still had not flinched.

"Pray to your angel," said one of them to Moultrie.

"For this moment, he has spared you." He and the others ducked behind some desks.

Moultrie grinned at the rhetoric, the Bahamian accents: reminders of the man he had destroyed.

Spoons's brace was rattling toward Moultrie across the blacktop. "My God! Moultrie, they're gunning for us!"

"Bluffing," Moultrie said, dividing his eyes between the Muslims and the guards. Putting some distance between his back and the Muslims, holding the .38 behind him. For a moment he stood considering the guards. "It's a fake."

"Ready," Freeman said softly into the radio that hung about his neck.

"Tell them this exactly," cracked the Warden's voice. "Tell them . . ."

"You gentlemen are to surrender in two minutes or you will be shot at random. Do you understand?"

Walsh was searching the hostages for Cays. He could not see him.

From up river sounded the great grinding and coupling of trains. Mill whistles marked time in another world. The Yard was silent beneath a cold drizzle.

"Go ahead," the Warden said.

Freeman turned to the guards, pulling out a pocket watch, cradling the shotgun in his left arm. "One."

Walsh swung his muzzle down to hip level. Did they have weapons?

Puffing on his cigar, Freeman did not take his face from the pocket watch.

*   *   *

"Moultrie, they're not faking," Spoons said.

"Take it easy."

From across the Yard: "You have sixty seconds, gentleman, or you will be shot at random," droned the big white voice.

"Brown!" Moultrie yelled. "Lace some shivs across a few of them honky throats!"

Childs hit the ground hard, felt his back sting as the breath exploded out of him. A black fist tore back his head and he felt against his neck the blade—thin, curved as the sharp day moon.

Freeman, slicing his eyes from the hostages to his men: "Two."

Walsh feels the cool, wet stock snuggling into his cheek. Safety catches are clicking off down the line. Steadying intakes of air. Bracing for the recoil.

"Thirty seconds!"

Suddenly from the right side, several prisoners are charging. Walsh swivels them into his sights and a clang rings out as Rhiner's barrel strikes his own from underneath, brings it into the air.

"Steady!" Freeman yelled.

"What's going on?" the Warden asked over the radio.

"Few guys broke loose, came over. Not enough."

Moutrie watched the Muslims receding along the walls, behind the guards, their hands in the air. Sticking his pistol into his pocket, he strolled out halfway between the sparse barricade and the guards. Half of the shotguns drew down on him. He turned his back to the firing line. "Whitie's bluffing. There ain't no bullets in those guns! And just look at our bad-ass Muslim brothers!"

The smile was spreading across Freeman's face. Turning to the line, slipping the watch away, shouldering his weapon. Then the radio began snapping: "Shut down! Freeman, shut down!"

"Weapons down," the Chief said, then yelled into the radio: "What the hell's the matter?"

"Governor's in it. Talk it out, he says. Get your boys out of there, Freeman. Get them up to the Arsenal."

When the guards pulled back, Moultrie laughed hard. He grabbed his belly, stooping down toward the earth, and laughed as hard as he could. Picking up whatever was about them, his brothers threw straight and fast at the retreating guards. Watching their thin white heads duck and shake, their white asses and legs scurrying back into the Tunnel.

The cold blade pulled away from Childs's throat, and his captor threw up his hands and yelled a long nigger yell as he danced with the others in the Yard. Childs rubbed at his neck, not realizing death had been so close. Watching the last of the guards slinking away, he felt a sense of relief at the guns that could not fire, the averted eyes. And all at once he found himself running with whites and niggers alike, tossing handfuls of concrete. Screaming: "You bastards! Ha! Ha! You silly ass bastards! Ha! Ha! Ha!" Throwing from his heart and guts at the retreating badges, the relentless stone, the awful repetitions of food and days and boredom.

Chief Freeman was waiting at the Yard door. Drawing coolly on his cigar, he regarded the Yard in silence, then withdrew into the Tunnel.

Childs was collared and herded back into the corner of the Yard with the other white men. "It was a nigger show and niggers was running it," someone said. "We just about got our goddamned throats slit because two niggers been playing tag with each other. You throw in Darcy, one spook burns the other, and the whole slammer goes up."

John Hawkins was kneeling beside a wounded man. He caught Childs's eyes, motioned him over. "Cays," Hawkins said. "Somebody busted him good in the head."

"Looks bad," said Childs, trembling because of the blood, because of Hawkins, too.

"When I hold up his head, slip these rags under it."

Childs did as he was told.

Hawkins wiped some blood off Cays's neck.

"He ain't dying, is he?" Childs asked.

Hawkins met his eyes straight on, then glanced at the new rhinestone.

Childs felt his hand going toward his ear. "Reckon I should take this out now."

"Why? You turn invisible without it?"

"Out here, with all these guys around—I thought maybe I should just get rid of it."

"Naw," Hawkins said quietly, nodding toward the cell blocks. "In there, that's where you should have thrown it away." He stood up, stared at Moultrie's men working in the Yard. "Maybe it don't matter though. Niggers or Freeman—one way or the other, we're going to get it."

*   *   *

224

The wind was tuning itself high and mournful through the barbed wire. Tall in the night, the guntowers were filled with sleepy men and guns, hidden whiskey, and bright kerosene lamps that fluttered and glowed like fireflies blinking through a smoked jar. Two of the main power lines were out. One remained to supply the great lights that now and again swept up a guard dog in the killing zone. A few fires burned outside the prison, where a detail of National Guardsmen had taken up positions. The air smelled of burning wood and damp stones and the long-boweled river.

Outside the prison near a guntower, Breen and White were warming themselves beside a fire.

"They just quit. Without a word," White said. "It was like their quitting triggered the riot."

"You got these things that happen to you sometimes," Breen said.

"All at once, the program just fell apart."

Breen avoided White's stare. "It's a tough break," he said—the recovered, miraculous strength of P. G. Carter, the sober eyes of Cowboy listing in his mind. The rain began again and he hunched his shoulders. "Just wondering what happened to Carter. He looked—better than the last time I saw him."

White was rinsing his hands in the firelight. "Fed him vitamins. Kicked his dead ass a little and stove him up on vitamins."

"All-state running back in high school, you know. He had the moves."

"He's still got them. Maybe you have to pry them out, but they're still sharp. Decked you pretty good."

"Slipped," Breen said quickly. "Grass was a little damp and lost my feet was all."

White smiled, turned his back to the fire, gazing toward the prison. "When you think they'll get some medical aid in there?"

"None coming."

"Some prisoners are hurt pretty bad, I hear. Couple steam pipes blew up. Fires. Some guys will die if somebody doesn't get in there."

"They put the chips on their shoulders."

"Sometimes I don't understand you, Father. There are some men suffering, dying maybe."

"They're not stupid. Somewhere they got a hole plugger."

"I took a medics course. Know a few things."

"Yeah—well, stow it. I got a feeling this thing will be over pretty soon. I got a feeling they'll need all the medics they can get in a few hours."

Walsh looked out across the dark buildings towards the Yard where the rioting prisoners had been contained. The rest of the population were securely locked in their cell blocks. He sat down next to Rhiner. "You know these guys pretty good. They wouldn't—torture Cays or anything like that, would they?"

"Might." Rhiner shrugged, stacking his shells on the floor of the guntower, which smelled of damp shoes and the static fire of the lamps. Three other guards stood near the south window.

Walsh resented the clipped answer. Settled back against the thin wall, listening to the other guards, who talked of hunting and sixteen-point bucks, of old war comrades and near glory, ending up with the beekeeper's death and how it foretold the riot.

"Hell of a thing you did for him too, Rhiner," one of them said, turning toward the lieutenant. "Piling all that honey around him. It was beautiful. It was the right thing."

Walsh started. Saw the secret smile in Rhiner's eyes.

A bitter squeaking of hinges and the trap door opened. "Heads up! Hot coffee and sandwiches coming." The cook slid the tray across the floor. "You boys hear what's going on in the Yard?"

Faces turning toward him, the cook jabbed a thumb over his shoulder. "Burning flags, them niggers. Broke into the mail room and stole it. Burning the American flag and drinking and screwing right in front of the fire down there!"

"Who says?" Rhiner asked.

"Freeman. Got it straight from the man."

"Sonofabitches!" someone said.

Another was holding up his hands. "It's alright, boys. Let them go ahead, them niggers." He slipped his thumb across his shotgun sights. "Come tomorrow the baker's going to get his pie back. Yes, sir!"

Walsh paid no attention to what was being said. Rhiner. Never had been able to figure his moves. Just a cold channel of ambition; but maybe not. He ate a sandwich, managed a couple of swallows of rank coffee. Checking his shotgun to make sure the chamber was empty, Walsh laid the stock between his legs, pulled his hat over his eyes. Thinking about his own intentions, about Peterson's death and what he could have done to prevent it; about Cays lying somewhere in the cold Yard. Around 1 A.M., he drifted to sleep. Seeing Patricia naked,

227

her arms opening for him, now barely hearing rain rattling on the roof, the tired, cracked swearings of the men, the worn jokes, long whiskey-sipping silences; shotgun between his knees, dreaming in the kerosene light shoals.

In the Yard, rain slapping against the tent made Moultrie even more uneasy, so that he drank now in gulps from a quart of Rayfield Jones's best buck. Like some thief or dark spirit in the marrow of his bones, the fear had arisen again. Poisoning his mind and blood, dieseling his heart. Questions festering in his brain like a swamp fever. An hour before it was so bad that he vomited. Now the bright whiskey was floating on his blood, holding the line and pushing back the darkness. Even so it was still there. Mixing his thoughts mad. Winding a dark horn through his brain.

Nearby, Spoons lay in a damp corner blowing his harmonica like some goddamned minstrel show comic. Clasping a large jar between his legs, Brown sat and gorged himself with peanut butter.

Moultrie turned up the roaring hurricane lamp. "You be ready tomorrow. Tomorrow they talk to us."

"They'll do more than talk. A minute ago, when Brown was burning all that canvas from the paint shop, I heard guards hollering from the towers. 'Them niggers is burning flags!' They're all really up for this, man. Just looking for a reason to kill us. Besides, what's there to talk about?"

Moultrie pulled his feet from a collecting pool of water. "About what we want."

Spoons wrapped some more newspaper around his brace. "And what is that?"

228

Feeling his heart quicken at the question, the darkness again unraveling, Moultrie took another sip and let the whiskey burn down his throat. "Freedom for our brothers. Fifty black men set free!"

"You're crazy," Spoons said, thumping the harmonica against his thigh.

"Damn you!" Moultrie lashed out toward him with an arm. "Don't you call me that. Damn you to hell! There's nothing wrong with me."

Spoons saw the spell flooding through his eyes again. "Sorry. Take another tug. It'll be alright now."

"Brown? Brown, you go get me Darcy."

Spoons and Brown glanced at one another.

"Leave him alone, Moultrie. He's got a tent to himself. It's a bad night," Spoons said.

"I want him here. I want him right here by me to touch."

Spoons nodded. Brown pulled a blanket over his head and went out into the rain.

"See these things, these spells came on my daddy too, after Mama died. He burned candles in the night. I can still smell them—the beeswax candles, hear him praying. But whatever was after him ate up his senses so he couldn't reason, couldn't team his eyes and brain. So they locked him up. They shut him away in the dark with his mind going to pieces on him like a rotting rag and he died there. Sometimes I get afraid it'll happen to me too."

"It's a fever on you, Moultrie. Hush now. Sip a little more."

"My daddy was a smack shooter. I never told you that, did I? No. But I don't hate him. Staying up there in that dark attic. Making over them rotting bodies. You

229

could hear him at night, smoothing away their secret whiskey wrinkles and sores. Pumping out their stinking syphilitic guts, saying: ''Scuse me, Brother Ralph,' and 'I'm sorry, Sister Anita,' and 'This won't trouble you much as it seems, Brother Ben.'" He took a long swallow. "That's why I'm going to get rid of dope and whores in this hell hole. That's why I killed the Muslim. It's ruining my brothers. It's corrupting my people."

Slowly a blanket was parting and quiet as night John Darcy appeared. Wrapped in an old coat, the strange black odor. Brown was not with him and Spoons curled tightly into the corner.

Rearing up on his elbows, Moultrie regarded him. "Angel of death." He smiled, rubbed his hands across his eyes. "Take some whiskey, John Darcy. Warm yourself."

In the hissing gas light Darcy seemed green, dark runnels of water slid off his coat. He squatted down beside Moultrie.

Rising with some effort, Spoons left the tent.

"Let him leave," Moultrie said, handing Darcy the jar while the room was blurring. He touched Darcy's face, studying it. Feeling easier. Feeling somehow that the fear should be inside Darcy, Moultrie stashed it in him like a jug and corked it up. Knowing that as long as he could touch it, see it, he would be safe. He lay back, letting the liquor wrap his bones warm like a shawl and felt his cells clicking off the light, pulling down the shade, acceding to darkness while another darkness prowled imprisoned within John Darcy.

Stooping down low, fingers testing the shadows before him, Father White edged carefully along the roof of

230

Building C, on his back a pack of medicines, bandages. He stumbled and fell, then recovered, now ready to dodge the searchlights. As he rose, he saw a dousing of lamps in guntower eight. The guards had seen him. He was scrambling toward the peak of the roof when he heard the blast and felt the impact square in the back. He started rolling down the roof. Tried to catch the gutter, but missed. Rushing darkness. And suddenly the wind burst out of him.

Just before the rain came down, Childs and the others took long pieces of tin from the shops and made lean-tos against the Industry Building. Hawkins distributed cardboard to place against the blacktop. After about an hour, Childs finally got to sleep, hearing a harmonica playing "The Tennessee Waltz" from somewhere in the Yard.

Near morning he was awakened by the scuffling of feet.

"For God's sake, don't let him kick off!" someone said.

As Childs moved out from the lean-to, he could see Hawkins kneeling over Cays, two or three men standing by.

Childs quickly knelt beside the guard. "Can I do something?"

"Put your hands in the center of his chest. Keep a strong rhythm," Hawkins said.

As he punched with the heels of his hands, Childs could hear a rattling, long and cold, from the shallow chest. Hawkins dipped his mouth down blowing hard, full into the washed-out face. Nothing. He pushed Childs away, once again heaving his own air into Cays, who suddenly convulsed so that Hawkins drew back. A black liquid ruptured from one of Cays's ears. Childs saw the eyes open to the weak light, then fill with darkness. Feeling his stomach roll, he ran to the side of a building. Felt his neck wring hard, but lost nothing from his belly. A while he stood, spasms still racking his stomach. Still seeing the ear's black coughings, hearing the thick, oily rattle. When his stomach quieted, he returned and found the body covered.

Hawkins sat in the new light, smoking. "You should have pumped harder."

"I was scared to break something."

"Fractured skull anyway."

"I saw brains run out his ears."

Hawkins pinched out his cigarette. "You should have waited on me. Red never would have touched you. Just a couple more days and Stuckey was burned chocolate."

"There was more to it, Hawk. Sixty cents an hour. I couldn't make it off that."

Hawkins ground his cigarette into the pavement. "No, I suppose you couldn't. I suppose none of us could. You just didn't know what to do about it."

"I ain't ashamed," Childs said.

They locked stares for a moment.

"Well, that's good, I guess. Anyway you can, you got to keep some kind of pride here. It's all that's left."

It was light now and the Yard began filling with noise. Sparrows piped in the gutters of the cell blocks.

"You go tell them niggers he's dead now. It'll mean something to them. Something real big. It'll mean ole Freeman's got what he wants to kill us all."

*   *   *

232

In the bright midmorning, when the Warden and Breen stepped out of the Tunnel to start their walk across the Yard, the prisoners began to jeer and boo. A tin can ˙ollowed by rocks whistled through the air. But the barrage was brief. Breen looked over his left shoulder. Along the rooftops Freeman was ready with fifteen guards, shotguns and Thompsons. Though the distance was only one hundred yards, it was the longest walk Breen ever took. When they reached the barricade, Brown motioned the two men on through and behind a tent drying in the sun, smelling of molding wool, and other things rusty and damp. Moultrie was sitting on a crate, paring an apple. Without looking up, he gestured toward two other boxes. Breen and the Warden sat down.

"Something you wanted to ask me?" Moultrie said, poking a sliver of apple into his mouth.

"No go, Moultrie. All of this. It's trash and no go," Breen said.

Moultrie raised his eyes, but said nothing.

"Close it down. You feel it. There's no way."

"Your beads are rattling, priest."

"Honcho this thing out and you get blowed away."

"Not before I make some honky stew."

Jesse Cates quickly stepped in. "I got your message about Cays. I want to know how he died."

"Banana peel."

"Look, you know what could happen here. Those guys on the roof aren't carrying squirt guns."

Moultrie nodded toward the hostages. "Those guys don't have candy canes across their throats either."

Breen and Cates turned. They considered the men a

moment. All seven guards had knives against their throats. The blades glinted in the sun.

"Alright, I'll tell you," the Warden said. "The food's crummy. The hospital's lousy. The visiting days are too short, right?"

Moultrie was smiling. "We expect you to act like savages. Treat us like swine. It's in your souls. What you're paid for."

Warden Cates crammed his hands into his pockets.

Breen was scratching violently at the back of his head, the blood rising at his temples.

Munching on another piece of apple, Moultrie shrugged, opening one hand toward them. "Half the guards smuggle in dope. The other half screw the cons. They are ruining my people."

"So?" the Warden said.

"So, you fire your flunkies and you get some honest men in here—black."

"What else?"

Breen snatched off his collar, clenching it in his fists. "Moultrie, get out of the goddamned Yard. You got too much gauge on you."

"As a gesture of good will I want fifty of my brothers released tomorrow, pardoned."

"Or?"

"I'll paint these walls with those filthy white bastards' blood," Moultrie said, throwing the apple core to the ground. "You think I'm not here for a reason?"

"You're a two-bit, back-stabbing coward," Breen said in a low voice.

"Watch your mouth, priest!"

"How many of your scum did you plant in that shower?"

"I cut out a tumor," Moultrie said. "And you and him and all the others are the reason it got so big."

"This will have to go to the Governor," the Warden said.

"Send it C.O.D. and let my people out by tomorrow."

"You know, Moultrie, I figure you could dump a lot of blood around this place," Breen said, rising, slowly moving toward him.

"Breen!" the Warden cautioned.

"Watch yourself, mother," Moultrie said, slipping his hand into his pocket.

"The Governor's not coming across for that crap, and you know it."

"Too bad if he doesn't. I got something of yours."

"You're just a bad little boy who needs his butt kicked," Breen said, again edging forward.

"Come on, two more inches."

Breen watched Moultrie's pocket. "Fingers," he said.

"Take it easy," said the Warden evenly.

"He's a punk," Breen was trying to judge the pocket.

"Don't you mean nigger?" Moultrie mocked.

"I mean punk!"

Breen felt the Warden's hand gently tugging. Then firmly. Back toward the barricade. "Any more of these guys get hurt—guard or prisoner—it's me and you, buddy!"

Moultrie shifted his attention to the Warden. "Twelve o'clock tomorrow, my brothers better be free or you're going to have a lot of dead screws."

The Warden waved away the two or three guards who watched through the closed section gate where the rest of the prisoners still lay locked in their cells.

235

"He rolled over you like pie filling," Breen said, kicking an empty box. This section of the Tunnel was still dark and cold with the morning wind. Pipes, wires stood ripped out from the walls.

"Think so?"

"He should take a couple, right in the gut. Acquire some humility."

"Would you kill him?"

Breen winced. "Pin his ears back. Spread his nose out a little bit maybe."

"Would you take a rifle and blow his brains out?"

"Sticks, Warden. The hell with Freeman. Go in there with sticks."

"Not against the pistols."

"What are you thinking?"

"Snipers."

"To pick him off?"

"Him and the other two."

Breen took a deep breath, closed his eyes, blowing out the side of his mouth. "Why the hell couldn't someone see this coming?"

"Moultrie's a shark and he wants blood."

"What about the Governor?" Breen asked, his eyes hovering on the Warden's face.

"By this evening he'll be ten bourbons away from the phone."

"Would you do something like this, Jesse? Kill a man—that quick?" Breen asked.

"I let my men go in there and it's fifty dead at least."

"I have to be against it."

"He said he had something of yours. It's White,

Father. He's got your boy. Couple of men spotted him from the towers."

"Oh, Jesus!" Breen said.

"Looked like he was hurt bad, I hear."

"The little punk said he was going for a drive. Get away from it, he said."

"Three shots and it's over," the Warden said, turning away. He climbed the stairs toward Carter's gate.

Breen picked up a bottle from the floor and heaved it against a wall.

Cays's death had hit Walsh hard that morning. At first he was stunned, then as the long day passed, he grew depressed trying to find some reason why the prisoners should murder Cays. Why any of this had to happen. Now in the early evening, his stomach burning from bad coffee, Walsh sat with the other guards just beside the main gate. Listening to Creekland recalling Cays's murder for the third time.

"Ole Langford, he didn't just let them do it, no sir. Slugged the hell out of one of them. Knocked dog shit out of him, I'm telling you. But then they pinned him down by them lean-tos in the Yard. And when they hit him with that pipe—oh, God, it was awful!"

"You see all this yourself, Creek?" Rhiner asked.

Creekland paled a little, seemed embarrassed. "Couple guys in the towers told me."

"Yeah," Rhiner said. "Yeah, Creek."

Silently stepping out of the shadows, Freeman stood before them, lighting his cigar. "Let's listen up!"

The men became still.

"The Warden says we hit the leaders. Moultrie and

two of his friends. Like chopping the head off a snake."

Cheers and applause.

"We do it sniper style. Three men, tonight, from the roof. I need good shots. Let's see some hands."

No one stirred.

"Why don't we all just go in there and have it out?" one man asked.

Freeman lit his cigar. "Some niggers got some of our buddies in there, mine and yours. One of them's already dead. Now I need three of you to end this thing. To stop any more murdering."

Walsh looked at Rhiner.

"Leave it alone, kid."

Walsh saw one hand rise cautiously, then a second.

"You pop one of those niggers and you'll last about two weeks in this place. They'll cut your guts out when it's all over," Rhiner said, his eyes intent.

Meeting his gaze, then letting his eyes wander, Walsh raised his hand.

"Okay. Let's go, Walsh."

Walsh rose, picked up his shotgun. Looking over his shoulder, he caught Rhiner's eyes, hesitated, then followed the others.

In the Arsenal Freeman handed out three 30-30 rifles.

"Which ones?" asked Carl Brantham.

"Moultrie, the runt in the brace, and the big boy. You hunt, Carl?" Freeman asked.

"When I was a kid."

"What'd you go after?"

"Deer, coons mostly."

Freeman grinned. "It'll be a good night for coon hunting." Turning to the other—tall, stooped. "How about you, Jake?"

238

"Frog gigging."

Freeman was still frowning a bit when he turned to Walsh.

"Squirrels," Walsh said.

The old face lit like a scrubbed pot.

"You know about squirrels?"

"They're quick. Got good eyes."

"You know where to place the round?"

"Head shot."

"I want it clean. I want to see a dead drop on Moultrie."

Walsh nodded, feeling a sudden heaviness in his limbs.

"You boys take the other two on the heart-lung angle. You fire and beat it. One shot." Freeman looked up, drawing long on his cigar. "We wait till full dark. You got the moon tonight. It's all you need."

Moultrie had piled up four or five wooden crates for a platform and placed two flaring lanterns beside it. He had decided to give a speech this evening; to reassure his brothers and let them know his plans. He was not afraid.

Under the brilliant moon, standing before their lost and confused faces now, he felt again the old excitement of the streets, of D.C. and Charleston. He began to speak soft and low.

"The Warden—today he came to see me. Wanted to know what I needed." Letting his eyes drift to the ground. In a quiet voice: "I said—freedom. I said justice. I said let my people alone."

The silent crowd, unsure, rustling.

"For a start, I said—get rid of those white screws. Let fifty black men be pardoned."

Brief applause, a rising. They moved closer.

239

Moultrie wheeled up, threw into his face whatever had been simmering in his heart for so long—love, love for all of them. "What we can do is bow our heads and say 'yes sir, Marse' and shuffle in to that hell hole back there and be spit on and whipped and God knows what else, or we can make the stand here and start building us a tower high as the stars, kicking white asses all the way up. And when we get there, when we get all the way up, we'll paint the stars black too, just like you and me, and we'll have our justice and our kind."

Faces now awakening.

"Brothers, this country is like a big, rich pond that's full and brimming to the neck. But whitie, oh, whitie now, he thinks he's the best fish and he thinks the pond was always his and he thinks that nobody can swim in the pond but him. Well, he swims and spouts and hurrahs in this pond and every time he comes across a different fish—brown or black or red or yellow—well, he just takes his ole broad tail and flips it up on the mud bank and lets it die."

Moultrie was making a tail with his hands behind him, swishing his butt, and the men were laughing. Then he leaned down into them.

"Listen here, people—this big white bass done gone too far. Let him throw away the red ones; let him stomp the yellow ones; let him beat on the eyes of the brown ones—but, oh Lord, when he takes hold of us niggers— by God, let him know that tigers ain't always striped and lions wear black skin! And then it's going to be us that's got a hold of him and we ain't going to let go till we chewed him up and his way of thinking and his way of living and his way of praying and drinking and screwing his rhythm and his style and his godawful white flour soul and spewed it out on that red pond bank for the flies and the worms and the wrath of the Lord God of Hosts!"

They burst alive in the Yard, screaming and cheering.

Moultrie himself felt free, high above them, only the tethers of their hearts binding him to this place. Now he let them settle awhile, then slowly began to weave back and forth, bringing up the rhythm.

"We've got something moving in us, spreading out, yes sir! Getting stronger, yes sir! And it's flooding out of the black deltas of the South, toward the black coal mines of Pennsylvania, across the black tar pits of the West— building, rising, roaring along the good, black roads of Watts and, like Dr. King said, I have a dream . . ."

The crowd roared.

"I have a dream that no longer will we rot and suffer in the white man's prisons; and no longer will we die of hunger and cold in the white man's ghettos; and no longer will the white man nail us on his cross of gold. Oh, yes, brothers, I have a dream that every black child can tear his face away from the ground and I have a dream that every black woman can use the moon for her mirror and I have a dream that every black man can raise his fist—high, high, high against the sun." Moultrie shoved his fist in the air and hundreds followed.

Heavily, carefully, he pulled his arm down, changing the fist into a palm, sliding it across his chest, then over his heart and then his eyes.

"And there will come a time, and maybe it holds its face to us now like a child waiting to kiss his daddy, when blood—blood must run. Blood must purify and set

241

back in place what has been taken from us. And let me see your hands now."

Mesmerized, raising their palms.

"Oh yes, those hands will set you free and be rich in blood and lift you up and be joyous in blood; and out of the whole world those strong hands, brothers, will make you a lasting and proud people by a tide of weak white blood!"

After Moultrie's speech, Childs saw two niggers carry a young white man into the "corral" as Hawkins called it. Childs did not know him, but a few of the other men seemed to. They called him Father and he told them about being hit in the back by a couple of shotgun pellets during the night. Moultrie had kept him all day asking questions about what was going on outside: what kind of guy the Warden was; how many National Guardsmen were positioned. The men changed the subject, then laughed for the first time in a while, recalling stories they had heard about a boxing match between Father and the older preacher. And Childs decided this must be the young minister he had heard men talking about outside the cafeteria—Father White. He seemed to be weak from his wounds now and asked for some water and food. The beans Moultrie's men had been carrying over ran out at lunchtime. But in the light from a big fire the niggers had just started, Hawkins found the last bucket of water and gave White a long drink. Childs knew it was hard for the men to part with the water for they had been rationing themselves nearly twelve hours now. Everybody was almost out, even the niggers. And Childs's mouth felt like a mud puddle licked dry by the wind.

During the afternoon some of Moultrie's men talked about giving up, going inside. Childs had heard a few say that they did not like Moultrie's way of doing things and that he had screwed up the prison good. Childs was hopeful the niggers would give up, but Hawkins said it was too late. He wished he could be closer to the nigger fire.

Moultrie had lit the fire for his brothers. The night was cold. The dry crates creaked and bickered in the flames like the bones of the dead on a frozen night. Moultrie let the soles of his shoes smoke, then pulled them back, enjoying the heat. He loved the smell of the bubbling pot, sharp odor of the last rotting tangerines, the smell of his sweating men. He had marched into them today, his brothers. Had set a thimble full of himself in every heart—freedom. And the fear that had so haunted him lately, tonight receded, like a dark polar tide. And all the promises made to himself, to others, had found fruition here and sprung to life from sterile prison stone. He was a leader. He had gathered them. No longer was it if I can, or when I can. It was upon him. Fifty of his brothers to be freed, the white guards thrown out! When he awoke this morning he could not fully yet believe that it was he who had brought these things to pass. And though he was satisfied, there was still one craving: to speak to his father. To sneak beside the great door and whisper into the room of the dead that all was well.

The 30-30 felt light in Walsh's hand. Toward the end of the roof he could see the flames of the fire in the Yard. Freeman motioned them down onto their bellies.

243

Cold tar pressing against his cheek and he slides to the edge of the roof, above the firelight below. Whispering in his ear, Freeman points out Moultrie. Walsh pulls the sleek barrel beside him. Solid stock settling into his shoulder. Not sighting down yet. Waiting. Hearing Freeman, his belt buckle scraping across the roof as he points out the other two targets. The moonlight is like a veil, like a frozen lake above the fire. And now easily throwing Moultrie's face down the barrel. Hanging it in the sights. Even from here the clear eyes and calm black hands. Now the last, gentle, shallow breaths—squeezing of the trigger. Noise, the blast, the smooth kick and Moultrie's head jerks to the left—brains and blood hissing into the fire. Hands too late bursting toward the already dead face. . . .

"Alright," Freeman whispered.

. . . Walsh awakened, brought himself back.

"On my command, pick them out nice and neat."

Moultrie was still laughing at Spoons's story, holding his hands on his aching belly, when he heard the reports. Saw Spoons as he suddenly grimaced, reached for his side, then fell to the ground, his bad leg twisting in the brace. And Brown gently slumping forward, the dull grin still on his face, dropping the peanut butter jar which shattered, quickly covered with blood from his chest. Diagonally overhead, Moultrie heard footsteps flying in the dark. He jumped up screaming: "Bastards! Sneaking honky motherfuckers! Two screws die tonight. You hear that? Two screws get hog-butchered tonight and more tomorrow! You sonofabitching honky murderers!"

*   *   *

Childs did not hear the niggers when they came and dragged away two guards. He was holding Hawkins' head, blood pouring out of the smashed skull. The Hawk's eyes very soft and quiet, still looking up toward the roof.

For the second day Walsh had not shaved. His beard crawled and stung under his neck. Sipping his coffee, he edged closer to the dying fire beside the main gate, stretching the cramps in his legs as the sun, red and cold, surfaced from the black river, still full of night and the smells of pine and palmetto. From a long way off he saw Rhiner climbing down from the guntower, his uniform wrinkled below his tired face and rough beard.

Stretching his shoulders, rubbing his palms together, Rhiner idled his eyes on the fire. "Rawls and Johnson, Moultrie's got them all stretched out. Seven o'clock he says, and then the others."

Walsh looked at his watch—six thirty. "He's crazy enough."

"Last night—they say the big one went down cold. Spoons took a good hole. Some hostage got plinked by a ricochet."

Walsh's plastic cup shriveled in the fire. "Freeman says I stay here, you know. Says I can't go in."

"Why did you pull the shot?"

"It was dark."

"You had the moon and that good fire."

"Not enough."

Rhiner stuffed a handful of shirttail into his pants. "The rifle was too light. You make mistakes."

Rhiner scrubbed a hand across his beard. "Sending all

245

three shifts in at ten till. The Guard hits from the rear."

"Freeman says when it's over I can punch out for good."

Pulling his hat brim across his eyes, Rhiner moved toward the Arsenal. Then he halted, half turned. "On the roof you should have done what you were there for. You should have blown Moultrie away. Two guys got their throats slit because you pulled the shot."

Near dawn Childs had promised one of the niggers a trick in exchange for a blanket. He covered up John Hawkins, and some part of himself, too. He folded the fine hands and closed the gray eyes and pulled the blanket closely over him.

During the night, when the two guards were screaming, Childs had shut his eyes, put his hands over his ears. Now in the crisp morning he looked at the bodies stretched out on the ground, necks slit wide open, draped over cinder blocks and much black blood. He did not feel sick or even sad. He did not feel anything now except the aching dryness of his throat and the cold wind.

"How does it feel?"

"Not good," Spoons said.

"There will be a doctor soon. They'll give us everything we want."

"Not if you kill two more screws."

"*Only* if I kill them," Moultrie said, still smelling the rotting blood of Brown, grinding it beneath his shoes into the blacktop by the sifting ashes of the fire.

"It hurts when I breathe."

"Breathe shallow."

246

"They're going to gun us down."

Moultrie smiled, piling back the big stones that now and again thundered down inside him. "When two more white chicken necks start bubbling red, the Warden will come across."

Walking back toward the prostrate guards, held motionless by the pistols of two young blacks, he noticed the tired quietness of his brothers. Could feel their cold faces, empty bellies. The air smelled of rust and ashes; of death. Moultrie squatted beside the guard closest to him.

"You want anything?"

Rawls raised his head a little, swallowed. "You got some water?"

Moultrie motioned to one of his men. "I want you to know why I'm going to kill you." He stroked his fingers across the pitted blacktop. "I hate you. All of you. I couldn't do it for any other reason."

One of the gunmen handed Moultrie a canteen. "There's no more. You going to give it to the screw?"

"We'll get water soon enough."

The chapel bells were tolling six forty-five. Moultrie pressed the canteen to Rawls's lips but he turned his head.

"Not to drink."

"Too late for a bath, man."

"I ain't been baptized."

Moultrie gazed at him for a moment, then pulled the canteen away.

"You could do that for me."

"They tell me it's quicker than you think using a knife. Like fainting."

247

"Just sprinkle a little on me. Say the words."

"I hate you, whitie. Those are the words."

"It's nothing to you."

Moultrie rose, turned his back studying the men, then looked at Rawls again. "I don't have the words."

"Make them up. Just a little water."

The water felt warm as he poured a palm full, flinging it into the white man's face. "You say what you need to."

"Moultrie!" boomed a big voice from across the Yard. Father Breen emerged from the Tunnel.

"Forget about them," Moultrie said to the two young gunmen stationed beside the guards. "The circus is closed!" he yelled back to Breen.

"White's got work to do. He's been here long enough," Breen said, moving forward.

Moultrie motioned the gunmen to keep their pistols out of view. "Those snipers your idea?"

"You forced it," Breen said, measuring out even, smooth steps.

"Can't hear. Come a little closer, priest."

Breen stopped, stared at the two blacks. "Martin Lee —it's time you and Pike got your asses into Mass."

"Sight down on him," Moultrie whispered.

The boys pulled out the revolvers but did not look Breen in the face.

Breen was moving forward, his eyes sharp, only twenty feet away.

"Now!" Moultrie yelled.

Nothing. Then, "He's a priest," one of them said.

Moultrie hesitated for only a moment. He hadn't

taken his eyes off the priest. Pike would be the closest. Now!

As Moultrie dove for Pike and the pistol, he felt a hand grab him by the neck, nearly lifting him off the ground, then slamming him back into the barricade.

Breathing heavily, Breen took the two guns from the boys and stuck them into his back pockets. Then he waded through the silent crowd of men to where White lay.

Waving both fists in the air, Moultrie began screaming, shoving into the men. "Kill him! Kill him, goddammit!"

The two guards had not moved.

Breen trudged back through the men, pistols bulging from his pockets, one arm wrapped around White's waist. Moultrie stopped screaming, slumped against the barricade.

Breen turned, gave Moultrie a hard once-over. "This guy's a two-bit punk," he said to the others. "In the Tunnel fifty guards are waiting to blow your guts out. For what?" He wiped a hand across his forehead and gestured toward the prison. "I'm telling you dumb sons-of-bitches to get back in that hell hole and do your time and light a candle. Get finished with all this—foolishness." Breen hooked his arm more firmly around White and went toward the Tunnel from where the guards were already filtering out into the Yard.

A pause, then one or two hands slowly raised. A few faces turned to Moultrie—nothing. More hands were going into the air. It was over.

Seeing ten or twelve guards sidling toward him, Moultrie dashed back through the barricade and ducked into the tent where John Darcy sat in molding darkness.

"Get me the priest. Promise me you'll get Breen! I got the dope stashed. You'll get it all," Moultrie yelled, just as the guards grabbed him.

John Darcy wiped at his sunken eyes, coughed like breakage in his chest. "A week," he said louder than usual. Then in a lower voice. "I got enough till then."

||| FOUR |||

I

TRAINS plundering the evening stillness, the cold hustling wind burning his ears, shagging leaves from the limbs of the November trees, bossing the swells of the river and the black frosting marsh grass. Walsh looked back toward the prison entrance. Heart gearing down slow and hard in his chest, arms and legs beginning to ease and uncramp. Propping up one leg on a step, he reached into his back pocket for the plug of tobacco. The taste was warm and refreshing, clearing the pressure of the long day which lingered about his eyes and cheeks. In the forward guntowers, covered trays of hot food were being hoisted to the guards by prisoners below. The pulleys were creaking and the tin trays flashing in twilight and the smell of hot cabbage floated on the wind. The riot seemed further away than just one week.

"Tough day," Rhiner said.

"Pretty rough," Walsh said, turning around.

"Had two escapes in the middle of it. Real crazies. You hear?"

"Saw their names today. Riker and Valànce."

"Jesus." He paused. "Feds are on their ass. No trouble there. But here—take us a couple months to get things cranking again."

"A long time."

"I saw bars bent in half. Locks laid open like egg shells."

"Took thirty minutes."

"Sonofabitch."

"Yeah," Walsh said, feeling a respect for Rhiner. An understanding. "Next week, Freeman says I punch out."

"I talked to the Warden. Told him you just blew the shot, pure and simple. He's for you."

"You did that?" The idea rushed him. For a moment he stood, puddled warm tobacco beneath his tongue. Stay. But did he have the strong blood to stay? Peppertown. "Two men are dead because I couldn't kill one."

Rhiner nodded, pulled up his collar around his neck. "You tuck it under your pillow at night. You wear it in the morning. You eat with it in the afternoon. On the roof, you got into debt. Where else can you go."

Walsh raised his eyes to Rhiner's. Saw a kind of acceptance and maybe something more. "How will it go here, me and you?"

"You bubbling? You tickled down in your gut about it?"

254

"Nothing like that."

"Something though."

"Something."

Rhiner shook his head and smiled and looked north. "River's high and running hard."

"There's talk of flood."

"There's always talk."

Moving beneath guntower one, Walsh could hear the ward keepers calling night Count from the dark buildings and the black river rolling toward twilight and the last birds singing from the trees.

||| 2 |||

THROUGH the first desolate night, Moultrie felt as if
light, as if legions of light, had collapsed and shattered
in himself, the tiny shards like coals sparkling, dying
in his belly, seeping into his lungs and spine, gathering
and collecting. Sucking at his soul like vicious night
barnacles, making his brain wheel and burn with the
knowledge—he had lost.

They had put him in the maximum security cells,
which lay to the left of the death house, outside the
main cell blocks. Stone walls three feet thick, sound-
proofed and padded; an iron shutter bolted across the
lone window, secured on the outside by a heavy pad-
lock.

The first day or two he had not eaten, feeling a deep,
gut-cramping contrition, mortification; as if some part

of himself, promised, had failed, had become diseased and needed to be cut out and burned to pure ashes. And this misery shoaled through his bones and dreams, through the bitter silences of the night and mean rustlings of the day until he knew that to survive he must fight against it. Unraveling the black roots of remorse and guilt, forcing himself to eat again, doing calisthenics, thinking of Spoons, seeking out worth again. And through this bleak purging of himself somehow the corpse of fear, which had stalked open-mouthed and stinking in him, dwindled into the stone, into the black eyes of winter rats. Perhaps all of this had taken place to rid him of his fear, to break free the cerements of the slack-jawed dead within him. To end the dreadful struggle with chaos. Perhaps this was victory and not defeat.

Now on the seventh day in maximum security there rose in him a keen brightness, relentless, clean and fresh as first ice—revenge, retribution. For in one week the angel of death had said that he would die—Breen—whom Moultrie hated so. Breen—whom he would like to pump full with his own bad blood, the weak blood that had failed. Pump the ugly white body tight with spoiled nigger blood like a slick, fat wood tick and then listen to the lovely pop of the knife as it dove into the shiny belly, spewing his own weak blood out of Breen's white body, before Breen's gutless and outraged eyes.

3

So John Hawkins was dead. . . . Childs had thought through again much of what Rose had told him. And in the past few days he had become more at ease with himself. Realizing what he could be, and what he could not. Coming to know what he was—a whore. Knowing, too, that he did not need Montana Red now. So after Count, in the evening, while Red was shaving his legs, Childs confronted him.

"I decided to get my own cell, Red. I'm putting in a request to the building sergeant tomorrow."

Red stopped shaving a moment, then began again. "I heard you went to see Rose just before the riot. Babe, you shouldn't let that faded valentine pour sugar in your ears."

"She talks good, but that ain't it."

"Flinks, babe, you still owe me, remember?"

Childs turned his back, climbed up to his bunk, and

sat down. "When I was little, growing up by the mill, I used to have a dream. Dreamed I had the best hands in the world. Better than the fanciest weaver. Dreamed I made slippers for beautiful young dancers. And it wasn't all a dream, Red. Rose helped me to see that. But I don't have to make shoes. I *am* the dancer. I am —Rose, now. And it makes me proud."

Montana Red sighed, toweled the remaining cream from his legs. "I've been here a long time, Danny. I know you have to make your own Easter baskets behind the walls. Let me know if you ever need my help." Red blew a kiss and climbed into his bunk.

Childs was surprised Red agreed so easily. He felt grateful and, lying down on his bed, began thinking what kind of present he would buy for Montana with his first money.

Montana Red had lain with Coot Pearson for nearly two hours. But Pearson had been here twenty years, appreciated the extra time, and would spread the word about Childs, who had just gotten his new cell.

"He's a molester," Montana said.

"The kid?"

"Got ten years for it."

"Aw, come on, Red."

"Took some little boy out in the woods. Did things to him there. Somebody said he carved a swastika into his ass when it was all over."

"That bastard," Pearson said, stepping into his trousers. "He was your boy though, Red."

"Just stayed with me. I didn't know till a couple days ago."

"Screwed his eyes out, I hear," Pearson said, smiling.

"I don't mess with molesters, babe. You know that."

"Yeah. Yeah, you're pretty clean," Pearson said, moving out on the tier. "What building is your boy in now, Red?"

"Four."

Pearson shook his head. "Cut a swastika into him. Jesus Christ! That's got a price coming, ain't it?"

Montana Red went into his cell. He had paid one of the prison clerks to doctor the records on Childs in case someone checked. Pretty boys were vain and bad. He promised himself never to touch one again. He took his temperature.

4

So he was fifty and getting fat. So what. It would work out—maybe. There was hope. Even here. Not much perhaps. Not for many, but there was always some, enough to work with; enough to let them chip away. *Laus tibi Christi.*

Breen was lathering in the shower, hitting the highest and best notes of "The Wind That Shakes the Barley" when the hot water shut off. For three or four minutes he was cursing so loud that even he could not distinguish the words. The next second he was out, into his habit, and pounding on White's door.

"I told you two months ago to fix that damned water heater. Now, what about it?"

"Tried," White said.

"You use a wrench, White. You got to have leverage," Breen growled, scrubbing his wet hair with a towel.

White nodded. Tightened the cincture about his freshly pressed habit. "How was the Provincial's letter?"

Breen shrugged, balled up the towel in his hands. "Up in the mountains, they got a place. Up in north Brazil. But the Provincial's playing footsy again."

"Good scenery, I guess."

"No damn bars and locks. No idiots running around burning buildings."

"A lot of sun, good wine probably."

"What the hell do you know about it? I've always thought that they should send you young guys out there. Let you learn what work is. Get a few gray hairs, then you can take charge of one of these—these lollypop factories. Up in the mountains, out in the missions— that's where you should be. Maybe they'll send you there."

"Maybe so," White said, unassumingly.

"Well, how's the shoulder?"

"Itches."

"Healing then. Good sign."

Moments later, scratching at his belly, Breen leaned against the doorjamb. "Look, Cowboy and some other guys want you to keep up what you were doing. So . . . you know, whatever they want."

White smiled. "Yes, Father."

"Another thing. I got an old friend coming by to-night—Father Tobias. Went to seminary together, a good guy. Oh yeah, he used to talk a lot of theology with what's-his-name—Merton. So you two can gibber about him all night. Anyway, Tobias is going blind and

262

got a dog and I hate dogs, so they bunk in your room and you get the couch."

"Sure."

"Another thing," Breen said, nervously rolling his cincture in his hand. "Tomorrow I'm rounding up some of these guys for confession. Going to chew ass in that little box. You want to give me a hand?"

"They could use it."

"Yeah," Breen said, glancing at White uneasily, flapping the towel over his shoulder, then halfway turning to go. "Oh, there's one more thing—I thought, you know, if you had a couple minutes . . ."

"I'll get the wrench. Fix it right now."

"No . . . no, it's not that. I just thought that . . . well, hell, I thought maybe you could hear my confession. Couple things I got to say."

"In the chapel?"

"No . . . it's good here." Breen stood straight, blessed himself, bowed his head.

"Just a minute," White said. He opened a closet, took out a stole, hung it about his neck, and gave Breen the blessing.

Folding his rough hands before him, clearing his throat, Breen began. "Bless me, Father, for I have sinned. . . ."

5

THE bowl of milk is warm, thick as porridge because of the white sugar. One week after his promise to Moultrie, John Darcy takes the mixture by trembling teaspoons while his bundled side and blurring mind work and pound for another sweetness and pure ending of pain. In the darkness, in the silent shadows of his cell, he lies upon the bunk, huddling the bowl against his sick belly while the hateful wind scratches and howls at his window. When the chapel bells toll eleven o'clock he is finished and kneeling before his cell door, arm extended through the bars, plying one of his instruments into the lock which springs like a trap.

On the first floor of Building One the lock securing the manhole opens and he slips down into a deeper darkness, into the damp sewer which leads to every major building of this prison though not outside of it. Here the small night lights glimmer before him like silver minnows. The guard will soon make his rounds again, but Darcy has long known where the light will go and where it will not. The darkest pools, the deepest troughs. Through the sewer there are other locks, screens, and doors, but they are old friends to him. Old faces that open and grin with a greeting creak. On his hands and knees now, the wet ceiling heavy over him, he creeps along, here and there resting, placing a hand against his throbbing side, pressing together the fresh bundle of rags, almost hearing his soft-footed brother cats who are following at a distance, grateful for their skill at baying the sewer rats.

Now, outside the chapel, he listens. Ears catching the sound of the dogs loose in the killing zone. He shudders. The rectory lock is stubborn. He hisses at it, curses. Thin hands like weasels fearfully wrestling with the lock beneath the moon, beneath the dull cancer in his side. In the rectory: full of smells that he cannot identify. Holding the ice pick against his bad leg. One hand before him in the dark. Moving toward the light at the stairs, the strange statue smiling above the flames of the candles. Wondering at this. At the white lady in blue, the small candles like night flowers blooming beneath her feet. Then the dark of the stairs. He is searching for Breen's room when he first hears it. Stops. Nostrils sifting the air. His ears pricked and cocked. Nothing. Carefully moves on thinking only his imagination. Again in the dark—clicking—paws. Now he can smell it, the dark hide, loathsome teeth and breath.

Out of the dark the dog leaps for his face. Instinctively Darcy thrusts, at once hearing a whine, then feeling a weight against him, knocking him down. Blood flowing down his arm from the filthy hide. In the half light the German shepherd's legs, eyes still twitching. Almost crying out he pulls himself away. Tugs the pick from the animal's chest. Turning back down the stairs— to Moultrie. Past the lady in blue. Wiping the animal's blood from his arm. Down through the rectory again —to Moultrie.

A sound awakened Father Breen, and he got up quickly to open his door. With a flashlight he searched the hall. By the plaster statue of an angel beside his door he found the light switch. Father Tobias' dog lay upon the stairs in blood. Bewildered, moving toward the dog, Breen could smell a strange, dreadful odor.

6

WHEN Moultrie first heard the ticking of the lock, he told himself the wind, and cautiously held his breath, trying to slow the beating of his heart, listening, until he heard a similar sound. Quickly he slipped out of his bunk, putting his ear against the cold iron window. Had Darcy come to tell him of Breen's death?

"Darcy?"

Silence.

"How is Breen?"

"How do you think? He sleeps."

"Did he see you? Did he know?"

"There were only candles in the darkness, brother."

"But did he cry out?"

"He could not."

"You did well, Darcy."

267

"Much better than you thought, brother. I have returned."

"Go to sleep now. Rest."

"There was much blood. Let me show you."

"Sleep now."

"Can you keep me out? Let me see you. Let me show you this blood."

Probably pride, Moultrie knew. He could understand such pride, but now there was something different in Darcy's voice. Was it the way he paced his words? "Do you have the weapon?"

Darcy paused. "Yes."

"You will not need it here."

"I have finished tonight."

"Leave the weapon outside and we will talk."

"I have put it away." Darcy slipped the ice pick into his trousers.

"Would you lie to me, brother?"

"I honor those who honor me. Are you so afraid?"

Moultrie stood away from the window. "Come in, brother."

The heavy lock twisted open.

Moultrie could feel the cell filling with the cold river wind and the night and the long, rank odor of the angel of death.

Moultrie was not afraid.

$\mathcal{V}$oices of the $\mathcal{S}$outh